FAITH, HOPE & LOVE

RACHEL HANNA

CHAPTER 1

There are days in life that a person never sees coming. Sometimes, those are good days, but other times they're not so good. Occasionally, they might even be surreal. For Faith McLemore, today was a very surreal day.

As she stood at the end of the long concrete pathway leading into the ominous brick building, she tried to assess how her life had gotten here.

Now almost in her mid-twenties, she expected to be at a totally different place. Traveling the world, working in fashion or maybe even politics, dating a handsome man with a strong jaw and even stronger work ethic. She certainly expected to have a big rock on her left hand by now, just like most of her other high society friends did. Even Eileen Lawrence, the most homely girl in her circle of wealthy friends, was engaged, albeit to an equally homely man. But he had money, lots of it, and that always made men more attractive.

Instead, she found herself in a very different stage of life - standing in front of this building, single, jobless and going in for a meeting she never expected to have. Yes, her life had definitely gone off the rails in recent months.

The death of her mother, Jane, had started the whole chain reaction of her life spiraling out of control. The sudden car accident that had claimed her mother's life rocked her world, but also her father's. He still hadn't recovered, and then he'd made his own poor choices in the years following that dreadful time.

As she approached the glass doors leading into the building, she steeled herself. Maybe it wouldn't be so bad. Maybe her visions of what this meeting would be like would be far off the mark. But as soon as she opened the door, she knew. The smells, the sounds, the energy of this place was unmistakable and worse than the nightmares she'd been having lately.

"Can I help you?" the woman behind the glass enclosed cubicle asked. Her face was impassable, and it seemed if she cracked a smile that her skin might actually split open.

"I'm here to see Jim McLemore," Faith said softly as she looked around her. It was like a foreign country, the dull roar of sounds she didn't recognize and voices she couldn't decipher. She pulled her expensive handbag closer to her body.

Sometimes she thought maybe she'd been too spoiled in her life. Her father and mother had made sure she had all the best. A big house, a pony as a kid, more family vacations than she could count, a brand new car when she turned sixteen. But that life was long gone, even though she refused to get rid of her expensive handbag. It was one of the only things she still had.

"Inmate number?" the woman practically shouted.

Inmate. Her father was now an inmate. Faith slid a small piece of paper through the window with the number written on it. The woman looked at it without speaking and printed a sticker.

"Put this on and go through that door. Take a seat."

Suddenly she feared the woman might slap an orange jumpsuit on her as soon as she crossed the threshold. There was something about being in an actual prison building that made her throat constrict a bit, and she wondered how her father was managing to put one foot in front of the other each day.

He'd only been there for two months now, but it seemed like an eternity. Aside from missing him desperately, Faith had lost the only home she'd ever known when the government had seized it as part of her father's assets. They'd taken just about everything at this point which was why she held her designer handbag so close. Well, that and the fact that she was well aware that criminals surrounded her at the moment.

She pulled her shirt sleeve down over her hand and turned the doorknob, noticing in her peripheral vision that the woman who'd checked her in was watching her closely and probably judging the fact that she didn't want to touch the doorknob.

"I'm a germophobe," Faith said, lying as she smiled at the woman. The woman didn't smile or respond and went back to looking at her papers, slightly shaking her head.

Faith walked through the door into a room with about ten small metal tables. Each one had two chairs across from each other. It was stark white with a smell she couldn't place. Maybe the aroma from what was probably a very nasty cafeteria?

She looked around at the families already having their visitation time. Mothers staring lovingly at sons, wives holding babies. There was an air of sadness, although everyone was smiling for the most part. This wasn't normal.

"Miss, you need to take a seat," a very large guard said as he towered above her. Faith nodded her head quickly and found the closest table.

There were no windows. The walls were concrete

blocks painted over with chips every few inches. The floors were some kind of 70's looking tile with flecks of avocado green. And her father lived here now. He would be living here for up to ten years, or maybe more. The judge hadn't gone lightly on him.

It was a far cry from their sprawling home near the city with its marble floors and huge swimming pool. Moments of her life flashed through her mind. Christmas parties with full orchestras right in her living room. Lucy, their live-in housekeeper, humming her made-up songs as she prepared four course meals in their state of the art kitchen. Getting her first car, a convertible, in their circular driveway. Her father had even placed a large pink bow on the top.

Her car had been confiscated, and last she heard, Lucy was working at a local diner slinging hash behind the counter.

Faith's eyes started to well with tears as she thought about the man she'd loved all her life sitting in some stinky cell for hours each day. What if someone attacked him? What if he had a medical emergency? Would they even help him? He was allergic to peanuts. Did they know that? Where was his epinephrine pen?

"Faith?"

She turned to see her father walking through another door. Faith stood, ready to embrace him after so many weeks, but a guard stepped between them.

"No physical contact."

"Come on, man. This is my daughter. I can't give her a hug?" Jim asked, looking up at the guard.

"No."

Faith swallowed hard and vowed not to cry. She didn't want her father worrying about her. He had enough to worry about.

"Hey, sweetie," Jim said as he took the chair across from her. Faith sat back down and smiled sadly at her father. He already looked different. Thinner. Pale. Darkness under his eyes that he only got when he wasn't sleeping well.

"Daddy. Are you okay?" she asked softly. She instinctively slid her hand across the table only to hear a grunt from the guard who was standing very close to them.

"I'm fine, honey. How are you?"

Faith took in a deep breath. "Not fine. My Dad is in prison, and I can't even touch his hand."

Jim nodded. "I'm so sorry, Faith. I really let you down."

She couldn't argue with that. He'd let her down in many ways. Embezzlement from his employer and federal tax fraud had put him where he was. When he'd gotten caught, he'd tried to cover his tracks, but he had done a sloppy job and made things so much worse.

"How are they treating you?"

"Actually, pretty good. Not as bad as I'd feared. My crime doesn't put me in the company of murderers or gang members, which is good. I'm in a different area."

"Oh, well, I guess it's just like a four star hotel then?" Faith said sarcastically.

"Honey, this is my home for a long time. I have to make the best of it."

"I know, Daddy. I just worry. I never saw you living out your older years in a place like this."

Jim let out an ironic laugh. "Yeah, me either. Let's talk about something else. How's Ted?"

Faith stilled in her seat. "He dumped me."

Ted had been her steady boyfriend for three years, but he'd broken up with her almost as soon as her father went to prison. Working at the same company as her father, he wanted no association with what her father had done. And truthfully, theirs had been more of a relationship of convenience than love. Still, right now she needed someone and she had no one. Everyone had basically abandoned her, not wanting to get the remnants of her father's misdeeds on them.

"That jackass," Jim mumbled under his breath. "I'm so sorry for all of this. I know I've said it a million times, but I wish I could show you just how much I'm sorry, honey."

Faith looked into her father's sad eyes. If she was

being honest with herself, she *was* mad at him. Mad that he'd chosen what he thought was an easier path to wealth than actually following the law. Mad that he hadn't considered her feelings when he'd hid money all over the world. Mad that everything was crumbling around her, and now she didn't have a mother or a father.

"He did it over text," she said of her breakup with Ted. She didn't know why she was telling her father even more information than he needed, but a part of her needed him to know that she was struggling. Putting on a brave face was a lot easier said than done.

"I don't know what to say, Faith."

She sighed. "There's nothing to say, Dad. It is what it is."

"Where do you go from here?"

Honestly, she hadn't considered that question. She'd spent the last few weeks moving into a crappy little apartment and putting out fires in her personal life.

"I have no idea."

"Have you looked for work?"

Faith chuckled. "Well, let's see. Who wants to hire a college dropout whose only work history includes being her father's personal assistant before he got put in prison for stealing money from his company and the United States government?"

Jim's face fell, and Faith suddenly felt terrible. It

dawned on her that he spent every single hour of every single day sitting in prison thinking about all the ways he'd failed her, and now she was piling more onto him.

"I'm sorry, Daddy. Gosh, this is all so hard." She put her head in her hands, wishing more than anything that he could take her into his arms and give her one of those hugs she'd so loved as a kid. How she would miss those hugs.

"I failed you miserably, honey. And I can never make that up to you…"

"Three minutes," the guard said as he approached the table.

"Wow, the time sure passed quickly," Faith said, looking at her watch.

"Faith, I need you to listen to me, okay?"

"Okay," she said, turning her attention back to her father.

"I called you here today because I want to give you something. Actually, it's something I should've given you years ago. You're going to need a pen and paper."

Faith pulled both out of her purse. Jim was talking fast, aware that the time was running out.

"I have a safety deposit box at United Federal. The one off Jackson Avenue. You know where that is, right?"

"Of course." Now she was getting worried. Had he hidden more money?

9

"The box number is 3459..."

Faith listened and wrote down the information as her father rattled it off.

"Dad, is this something I can get in trouble..."

"No, of course not sweetie. But that box is your future. It's how I think you can get back on track in your life. Make no mistake; it's going to be shocking. And maybe you'll never want to see or talk to me again, but I can't go on without you knowing..."

"Time's up," the guard said as her father stood up.

"I don't understand, Dad."

"I love you, Faith. Just remember that, okay?"

He slowly walked away with the guard until Faith could no longer see him in the window, and she was left to wonder what other secrets her father had been hiding. Would these shatter her world into a million pieces like his last secrets did?

～

"Miss McLemore? I'm Constance Arnold. One of my tellers said you're here for a safety deposit box?"

"Yes. I have the information right here." She handed the piece of paper to Constance.

"Great. Follow me, please."

She followed behind the woman into a small room off the main banking area. There was a nondescript wooden table sitting in the middle of the room, surrounded by walls of shiny safety deposit boxes.

Constance unlocked one from the wall and placed it on the table. "Take all the time you need."

Faith just stared at the box for a long while, her hands shaking in her lap. Why would her father be so secretive and not just tell her what was in the box when she visited him? Why keep her in such suspense over a whole weekend until the bank opened again?

She slowly opened the box, prepared to find any manner of illegal material or stacks of hidden money. Instead, there was a simple white envelope and a file folder. Almost not worth paying for a safety deposit box.

The envelope had her name on it, written in her father's unmistakable handwriting. She rubbed her fingers across it for a moment, trying to feel any connection to him that she could. His cologne wafted up from the box, and she brought the envelope to her nose. She missed him. Things would never be the same, and thinking about that made her sick to her stomach.

One day, she might get married. Have kids. But her Dad wouldn't get to walk her down the aisle or hold his firstborn grandchild. She felt sad and mad at the same time.

"Stop it, Faith," she said to herself. Refocusing her mind, she stared down at the envelope in her hands, took a deep breath, forgot to let it out, got light headed, finally exhaled and then opened it.

To her surprise, only one piece of paper was inside and it was all in her father's handwriting. He rarely wrote long letters like this; mostly he'd just signed checks and report cards over the years.

Dear Faith,

If you're reading this letter, something went wrong in my plan to change our lives. I want you to know that I always tried my best for you. Being your father has been the greatest joy I've ever known, sweetie. But now I have to tell you something that may forever change our relationship because I know it's what's best for you.

I am not your father.

Faith's breath caught in her throat as her heart began to race. What? He wasn't her father? She struggled to take her next breath, positive this is what a panic attack must feel like. Steeling herself, she continued reading.

I know this must come as a shock to you, but it's true. Your mother and I kept it from you when you were little because we didn't want to confuse you. But when she died, you were all I had in this world and I couldn't risk losing you. So I continued to lie by omission.

Your biological mother was young and in a bad situation, from what we were told. She couldn't take care of you, and at the time your mother was volunteering at a crisis pregnancy center. Your mother gave birth in Virginia, and we got the call from one of our connections at the adoption agency. From what I understand, she went home afterward and finished school.

So now I have to give you back to your original family, Faith. It's the only gift I have left to give you - a chance at being a part of a real family and having somewhere to belong in this crazy world.

I adore you, my sweet girl. Always know that. I wish I'd been strong enough to tell the truth and not keep secrets, but I wasn't. You were too special to me, and I kept you to myself. And I don't regret a moment of being your Dad.

I love you, honey.

Faith shook in her seat. She felt a swirl of emotions come over her. Anger. Shock. Sadness. Grief. Confusion.

Jim McLemore wasn't her biological father. And her mother hadn't been her mother. Her brain hurt.

"Miss McLemore, are you alright?" the woman asked as she came in to check on her.

Faith's face was red, her eyes full of tears. She eked out a few words. "Yes. I'm fine. Just a little emotional." The woman nodded and walked out, although she still had a look of concern on her face.

Faith reached down into the box and pulled out the file folder. There wasn't much in it aside from her birth certificate, which listed Jim as her father - and another piece of paper.

On it, there was random information written including her birthdate and a town in Georgia. Faith had lived in Virginia her whole life, so she knew no one in Georgia. Well, until now, apparently.

"January Cove," she said to herself as she pulled out her phone and did a search. Looked like it was a small beach town near Savannah, and it honestly looked like a great place to escape to right about now. Staying at a hotel or even a B&B would be a lot better than her current ratty one bedroom apartment near the prison. God, her life was a mess.

But first, she had some questions for her father.

~

"MA'AM, I told you. This inmate has specifically requested not to receive a visit from you at this time."

"Can you please talk to him for me? I need to ask him some questions. It's very important."

"No, I cannot. Maybe try writing him a letter?"

Faith hung her head and walked away from the window. Why would her father block her from visiting? How could he drop a bomb on her like this and then hide in his cell? None of this made any sense to her.

As she walked to her car, she thought about how her life had seemingly blown up in front of her. She'd lost her mother and now her father. Her boyfriend had dumped her. Friends had scattered, no longer taking her calls or meeting up for their weekly lunch dates. She was flat broke with just a small savings account to start her life over.

And yet none of those things had been in her control. That's what made it so hard to stomach.

"Well, fine, Dad. Don't talk to me," she muttered as she started her car. She sat there for a moment, staring at the prison. "I'm so mad at you," she said through tears. "But I love you, Daddy. Be safe."

And with that, Faith decided to leave Virginia and head to January Cove to find some answers one way or another.

CHAPTER 2

aith pulled into January Cove on fumes, too tired to stop at the gas station and not realizing there wasn't going to be another one for miles. Driving her "new" beat-up compact car hadn't been nearly as comfortable as she'd hoped, but at least it had gotten her there. As she parked her car in front of Addy's Inn, the place where she'd made reservations, she was struck by the quaintness of the small beach town.

Virginia had always been her home, but she could see how people would want to live in this place. It was smaller than she was used to, but cute and wholesome looking, like out of some 1950s storybook.

Still, she already missed the mall. Faith had always been a social butterfly, flitting between events and shopping excursions. Her father had spoiled her something fierce, even into adulthood. It was hard to believe that those days were over. She didn't know any other way of life.

The Inn was cozy looking and definitely historical. She stepped out of her car, her overnight bag slung over one shoulder and her suitcase in her other hand, and locked the door.

January Cove was cute, but it was a far cry from the big city. She doubted that there would be any upscale boutiques or private tennis clubs here. It was just as well since she was flat broke and her short-term rental would use up the rest of what she had in savings. Still, she had a reputation to maintain, even if she was the only person she knew in this town. Maintaining her dignity was important; at least that was what her parents had always taught her.

As she walked down the sidewalk toward the set of stairs leading up to the grounds of the Inn, she was suddenly knocked off her feet by a large furry animal. She hit the ground sideways, her expensive suitcase flying over her head. The animal, which she had now identified as a fluffy dog of some kind, was licking her face and wagging its tail.

"Scooter! Scooter! No!" she heard a man yelling in the background. Suddenly, Scooter flew backward and she could see the sky again. And a man with a worried look on his face. A very handsome man, actually.

"Are you okay, ma'am?" he asked, kneeling down beside her.

"I... I think so," she stammered. But she wasn't totally okay. Her knee was hurting pretty bad, like those times she had scraped it riding her bike as a kid. Those times when her father had tended to it. *Her father.*

"You're bleeding," he said, looking down at her knee.

"It's fine. I just need to..." she started to stand up, but she felt light headed so she laid back down. "Is the street moving?"

"Uh oh. You might've hit your head. I'm calling this one in."

She had no idea what that meant, but soon she heard him on the phone. The dog was now tied to the lamppost.

"I'm so sorry," he said once he hung up. "Scooter gets a little excited when he goes for a walk."

"Yeah, well maybe you should keep better control of him then," she growled. Her knee was burning, and although the lightheadedness seemed to have passed, she wasn't about to chance getting up again.

"Noted."

"OH MY GOODNESS, ARE YOU OKAY?" Faith heard a female voice behind her. The woman knelt down on her other side, a concerned look on her face.

"Well, I've been better," Faith muttered.

"Of course," the woman said with a sad smile. "What can I do?"

Now the man was standing up, looking down the road impatiently as he held the leashes of at least three dogs that she could see. She watched him for a brief moment and couldn't help but notice how good looking he was. But then the pain in her knee took over the part of her brain that said staring at strange, albeit sexy, men wasn't top on the list of things to do right now.

"Maybe help me sit up and lean against the wall?" Faith finally said.

The woman helped her scoot backward and get her back against the cold rock wall. Faith took a deep breath as she tried to straighten her legs in front of her.

"Here," the man said to the woman as he pulled his sweatshirt off, revealing a tight gray t-shirt underneath, and tossed it to her. She rolled it up and put it under Faith's hurt knee.

"I'm Addy," the woman said, obviously trying to make small talk while they waited for something. She wasn't sure what they were waiting for exactly.

"I'm Faith. Wait, Addy? As in the owner of this inn?"

19

Addy smiled. "The very same one."

"Well, this is ironic. I'm your new guest."

"Miss McLemore?"

"That would be me."

"I'm so sorry. How did this happen?"

"It was my fault. Scooter got away from me," the guy said, his face contorted in pain. Or maybe embarrassment at his inability to hold onto his enormous, slobbery dog.

"Scooter can be a handful," Addy said. Just then, Faith heard the sound of a siren screeching down the street.

"Oh dear Lord. You didn't call an actual ambulance for a skinned knee, did you?" Faith asked.

The man smiled. "Better safe than sorry."

"A bit dramatic, don't you think?"

"You were dizzy just a few minutes ago. I'm not taking any chances. Could be a concussion."

"I didn't hit my head."

"Or whiplash."

"My neck feels fine."

"Hard headed much?" he asked, a hint of sarcasm in his voice. Addy giggled under her breath.

"You two sound like an old married couple." When she didn't get laughter from either of them, she cleared her throat and stood up. "Why don't I take the dogs?"

"Thanks," the guy said, handing the leashes to Addy before walking toward the ambulance.

"Don't worry. Brandon will take good care of you," she said with a smile before walking back toward the inn, pulling on multiple leashes as she led them up the stairs.

"Wait, what?" Faith said, but Addy was already out of earshot. Okay, so good looking dog walker guy's name was apparently Brandon.

"So what happened here?" a young paramedic asked as he walked up with a large bag slung over his shoulder.

"Well, I was walking like a normal human being when a large furry animal knocked me down. Apparently the dog walker isn't great at his job," she said, her teeth gritted as the pain set in. Her knee felt like it was literally on fire.

"Dog walker..." the paramedic said with a confused look on his face as he looked over at Brandon.

"Yeah, apparently Scooter is a mastermind and I didn't know it," Brandon said, cutting the paramedic off.

"Let's take a look at that knee," the guy said as he gingerly slid her loose fitting yoga pants up her leg to reveal a pretty nasty skinned knee.

"Ouch ouch ouch..."

"Sorry. I'm going to clean this up and then I'll put something on it to deaden the pain a bit, okay?"

She nodded her head and closed her eyes. Her pain tolerance had always been low. Paper cuts were enough to send her over the edge most of the time. And now she had a skinned knee and torn yoga pants. And these were her last pair of the expensive kind. The last vestige of her old life.

A stray tear rolled down her cheek. Not because of the pain, but because of the loss. She was in a foreign place with people she'd never seen, and everything she'd owned was basically gone. Right there in the middle of the main street in January Cove, she felt naked and exposed to the whole world.

"You okay?" Brandon asked as he knelt beside her while the paramedic ran back to the ambulance to get the spray.

Faith looked over at him. "Um, not really. This wasn't in my plans for the day."

"I don't know how else to say I'm sorry."

"Look, you can go on home. Rescue Addy from your unruly dogs, okay? The EMT will patch me right up and we can both move on with our lives." She leaned her head back and sighed. The paramedic, whose name she still didn't know, came back with a very cold spray and coated her sore knee. Within a few moments, the pain had lessened greatly.

Brandon didn't respond to her request for him to leave, but instead turned his attention to the EMT. "We need to transport her to the ER for observation.

She almost fainted, and I want to be sure she doesn't have a concussion."

"Excuse me, sir, but I don't need you requesting medical services for me. I'll be just fine. I certainly don't need a big bill from the ambulance company."

Brandon smiled slightly and looked at the EMT. "I'll transport her in my Jeep then."

"Um no, I won't be riding with a complete stranger."

Brandon looked at the paramedic and smiled. "You can trust me, I promise."

"Isn't that what every serial killer says to his victim just before he throws her in the trunk of his beat up compact car?"

"Wow, that was a little specific. Listen, Joe here will tell you I'm trustworthy. Plus the hospital is literally three blocks away."

Joe. The paramedic's name was Joe. How incredibly basic, she thought to herself.

"Ma'am, I really do think you need to be checked out by Dr. Becker. He's our ER doctor, and he'll get you in and out quickly," Joe said, smiling at her with his perfectly straight, white teeth. She was almost sure he was a Boy Scout at some point in his past.

Faith sat for a moment and stared back and forth at the men. Maybe they were right. Her head was hurting a little, and she didn't want to start her trip off by dying.

"Fine. I'll ride with you."

"Great. Let me just take your bags up to Addy. She can get your room all ready for when you get back."

"Wonderful," Faith said with her voice dripping in sarcasm.

~

THREE BLOCKS WAS a long ride when the woman sitting next to you was ticked off and nonverbal, but Brandon was going to try his best to make her smile.

That was his personality. He wanted to see people happy. Sometimes that had been his downfall, but today it was his focus. Make this very uppity woman who was obviously not from around here actually crack a smile.

"So, where did you come from?"

"What?" she asked, staring straight ahead at the road.

"You're visiting January Cove, right?"

"Well, yeah, seeing as how I was checking into Addy's."

"Right. So are you here for business or pleasure?"

She sighed. "Do you always talk this much?"

"Yes. Most people like it."

"Really? Interesting."

Again, she stopped talking. Thank God they were almost there. He'd get her out of the car, make sure she saw the doctor and didn't sneak out the back door, and get back to his house before dark.

"Not a dog lover?"

"Actually, I like dogs when they're well behaved."

"Well, dogs are like people sometimes. They just get excited and overwhelmed with enthusiasm."

She chuckled under her breath, but it wasn't a happy laugh. More of an ironic one. "I wouldn't know."

Her response made him sad. No. He wasn't going there. It wasn't his job to make this bitter, strange woman happy.

"Here we are," he said as he pulled up to the ER door.

"Great. Thanks for the ride," she said as she quickly grabbed for the door handle.

"I'm coming in with you."

She turned to him, her eyebrows stitched together. "No, you're not. That's where I draw the line."

"You don't need to be alone. In a medical setting, you should always have someone…"

"If I say okay, will you stop talking for awhile?"

Brandon ran two of his fingers across his lips as if he was zipping his mouth shut. He knew it wouldn't last.

Faith hobbled into the ER and walked up to the desk, Brandon hot on her heels.

"Reason for your visit?" the woman asked from behind the counter.

"I was run over by this guy's unruly dog and hurt my knee," she said, cutting her eyes at Brandon. He smirked.

"Possible concussion as well. She was faint at the scene. Wound was dressed by Joe. Stitches weren't required."

"Why do you use so many words?" she asked shaking her head.

"Name?" the woman asked.

"Faith McLemore."

Faith. That was her name. He realized he hadn't asked yet. She didn't look like a Faith. Maybe a Tiffany or a Heather, but not a Faith.

Even after toppling to the ground and getting a banged up knee, she was a beautiful, well put together woman with nice, designer clothing and one of those luggage sets you'd see advertised in a high end travel magazine.

She just didn't feel like a Faith.

"You can bring her back to the triage room, Brandon," the woman said. Faith looked at him confused.

"Why does everyone seem to know you?" she asked as he led her to a back hallway.

"Small town," Brandon said, shrugging his shoulders.

FAITH LEANED back against the hospital bed, her knee elevated on a rather flat pillow. What was this guy's deal? Why was he so well known and interested in the status of her health?

By far, this was the strangest little town she'd ever visited.

Brandon had finally left her alone for a moment. She closed her eyes and took in a deep breath, trying to summon the calming energy of her former yoga teacher back home.

Coming to January Cove to try to uncover her past had been hard enough, but to start her trip this way had deflated her in so many ways. Maybe it was a sign from the Universe that she should go back to Virginia and leave well enough alone.

"Dr. Becker will be in shortly," a nurse said, poking her head into the doorway. Faith nodded and leaned back again.

She'd just wanted to unpack her car, get settled in her room and devise a plan to figure out where she came from.

The information her father had given her had been sparse to say the least. Just the name of a town and the possible age of her birth mother. That wasn't a lot to go on, especially since she didn't even know if she was born in January Cove in the first place.

In the two weeks since she'd been to see her Dad,

she'd called, tried to visit again and written a letter that was returned to her. It was hurtful and frustrating.

The father she'd known, the man who had taken her to father-daughter dances and out for ice cream sundaes (on Sunday, of course), was a stranger now. She didn't know this person, this "new" man who would abandon her when they both needed each other.

For the first time ever, she felt truly alone in the world. No Mom. No Dad. No boyfriend. No real friends.

If she kept up this way of thinking, the ER doctor might just transfer her right over to the mental hospital.

"The doctor hasn't come in yet?" Brandon asked as he pushed back the flimsy curtain that was separating her from the rest of the truly sick people in the ER.

"Nope. Not yet."

"He should be here soon. Dr. Becker is a fantastic physician. He retired here about twenty years ago from Chicago."

Faith laughed. "He came from Chicago to this place?"

Brandon eyed her carefully. "Believe it or not, a lot of people choose to move here. It's a wonderful place to live and raise a family."

Faith shrugged her shoulders. "To each his own, I

suppose."

"Okay, so what is your idea of a great place to retire to then?" Brandon asked as he sat down in a chair next to the bed.

Faith thought for a moment. "The south of France. A villa beside the aqua blue water. A full housekeeping staff, of course. And a personal vegan chef familiar with the local cuisine."

"Wow, that was also oddly specific. You're vegan, huh?"

"I am."

"Don't you ever miss a nice juicy steak?" Brandon asked, a grin on his face.

"Are you trying to start an argument?"

He sat back and sighed. "No, not really. But you do strike me as the type who likes to argue."

"Oh really? And you know so much about me, do you?"

"I know your type."

Faith seethed. What right did this guy have to judge her based on the little bit of time he'd known her, especially since he was the reason she was sitting in the ER in the first place.

"You don't know as much as you think you do," she said, leaning back with her arms crossed.

"Sorry for the delay," Dr. Becker said as he pulled back the curtain. "Had a little emergency with a nursing home patient. Faith, I presume?"

The older man was tall and thin, his thick head of white hair looking like fresh snowfall had landed.

"Yes."

"I hear you took a tumble after Scooter got a little out of hand..."

"I'd say out of hand is an understatement," Faith said. "Brandon here apparently doesn't have a very tight grip."

"Faith..." Brandon started to say.

"I mean really, who has a dog they can't control any better than that? My clothes are covered in hair and slobber. Do you know how much this sweater cost? It's cashmere!"

She found herself getting more and more irritated by the entire day. This wasn't how she planned for this trip to go.

"Miss McLemore, I..." Dr. Becker started to say.

"I really should sue, you know. I'm probably going to have a scar, and I like to wear skirts in the summer!"

Now she was embarrassing herself. But she couldn't stop talking. This guy just got under her skin and all over her nerves.

"But you don't understand..." Brandon said, standing up and trying to get her to stop talking. But if Faith McLemore was anything, it was stubborn as a mule.

"And what if I do have a concussion? That could

affect me for life. And for what? Because your big oaf of a dog couldn't resist tackling me?"

"Miss McLemore! Please!" Dr. Becker finally shouted. Faith stopped, stunned by his booming voice, and took a breath.

"I'm sorry, Dr. Becker. You didn't deserve to hear all of that."

Dr. Becker exchanged glances with Brandon, as if they had some secret between them.

"What?" she asked.

Dr. Becked sighed. "Miss MeLemore, Scooter is actually my dog."

"I don't understand."

"Brandon here was doing me a big favor by taking my dogs out today. I got caught up here at the hospital due to a car accident emergency last night. I've been here for almost eighteen hours, so Brandon was just helping me out."

"Oh."

"I'm very sorry about what Scooter did. He's really a very sweet dog, but I just adopted him two months ago from the shelter so he's still learning…"

"I understand…"

"I will definitely cover all of your medical costs, and if you'll tell me where you got that sweater…"

"Dr. Becker, no, don't worry about my sweater," Faith said. "I'm sorry. I've just had a very bad couple of weeks, and I took it out on you."

"No, actually you took it out on me," Brandon interjected.

Faith glared at him. "Why are you still here exactly?"

Dr. Becker chuckled. "You two sound like an old married couple."

"An unhappy old married couple maybe," Faith muttered under her breath. "Thank you for explaining things, Dr. Becker. I'm sure this was just a fluke accident."

"Oh, don't worry. I'll be enrolling Scooter in obedience school on Monday morning," he said with a smile. "Plus, I'm about to take a nice week long vacation, so I'll have time to work with him. Thankfully, Brandon here will be taking my shifts so I can get some much needed time off."

Dr. Becker turned around to wash his hands in the nearby sink as Faith turned to look at Brandon.

"You're taking his shifts? But…"

"Now you're putting two and two together. Yes, Faith. I'm a doctor here."

Faith's mouth dropped open. "I…"

"Might want to close your mouth. Lots of germs floating around this place," Brandon said with a wink.

"Dr. Becker, radiology is on the phone," a nurse said, poking her head around the curtain.

"Oh goodness, I've been waiting for their call. Miss McLemore…"

"No worries. I'll be here when you're done."

Faith sat still on the end of the table, her hands in her lap. Finally, she broke the silence.

"Why didn't you tell me you're a doctor here?"

"Didn't have much of a chance. You are kind of difficult to talk to, Faith."

Faith laughed under her breath. "I'm actually a lovely person. I've just had some challenges lately."

Brandon smiled. Man, he did have a very nice smile. "I get it. I don't judge anyone based on first impressions anyway. Maybe we can start over?"

"Well, you and Addy are officially the only people I know in this town, so I guess I can't afford not to give it another shot."

33

CHAPTER 3

*a*fter several hours at the hospital, Faith was finally released. The sun had set long ago, so Brandon wouldn't let her walk back to the inn. Besides, her knee was still hurting, she had a dull headache (no concussion though) and she was starving. The vegan breakfast sandwich she'd eaten in the car that morning wasn't exactly doing the trick anymore.

"Are there any vegan restaurants around here?" she asked Brandon as they walked to the car. She tugged on the plastic hospital bracelet on her wrist and tore it free, tossing it into a nearby trashcan.

Brandon chuckled. "In January Cove? Not that I know of. But, if you want fried catfish or biscuits and gravy, we've got you covered."

"I'm sure you do. I was hoping for something a little more... healthy. I mean, you're a doctor. Surely you know that a plant based diet is better for your body and certainly better for the planet."

"Maybe so, but I'm also aware that while I want to live a long life, I also want to live a happy one."

Faith smiled. "And biscuits and gravy make your life happier?"

"Immensely."

Brandon unlocked his SUV and opened her door. Faith climbed inside.

"So I take it you're hungry?" he asked as he slid behind the steering wheel.

"Very. But I'm sure Addy has something I can eat."

"Actually, there is a nice seafood restaurant down by the water. I'm sure they have salads and so forth. Want to give it a try?"

"I'm kind of exhausted. Not sure I want to do the whole fancy restaurant thing."

"Okay, I have an idea if you're game?"

Faith was far too hungry to argue. "Sure. What's the idea?"

"It's a surprise."

"Great," she said rolling her eyes. "So far I love your surprises."

~

BRANDON HAD no idea why he was doing all of this. As he rushed around the small grocery store, he wondered why he was trying so hard to impress a woman he barely knew and who seemed to despise him.

But here he was.

"A vegan sandwich?" the man behind the deli counter asked. "You do realize that we cut meat and make subs here, right?"

Brandon forced a smile. "Yes, Tommy, but I need something without meat. Like maybe lettuce, tomatoes, onions... and some of that vinaigrette everyone talks about."

A few minutes later, Tommy had created a vegan masterpiece. Brandon grabbed a fruit tray, some sparkling water and some disposable cups.

When he arrived back to his vehicle, Faith was sound asleep, her head leaned to one side. He stopped for a moment and watched her through the window, her chest rising and falling. She looked peaceful, and he hated to wake her up.

For a moment, he wondered about her life. Where had she come from? What was so wrong that she kept mentioning? And why was she in January Cove in the first place?

But Faith didn't seem like the type of person to open up easily. She seemed walled off, hurt by something or someone.

"Don't try to figure it out," Brandon whispered to himself as he walked around to the driver's door and slipped inside. Faith stirred as he carefully placed the paper bag behind his seat.

"Did I fall asleep?" she asked, her voice still groggy. She yawned.

"Seems that way."

"How long was I out?"

"Just a few minutes."

Brandon pulled out of the parking lot and headed toward their destination.

"It is always this cool at the beach?" Faith asked, crossing her arms.

Brandon laughed. "Not usually, but sometimes it can get a little crisp during this time of the year. Here," he said, reaching into his backseat for the extra jacket he kept.

"Thanks," Faith said, surprising him by not saying no to wearing his clothing. Maybe he was making some headway with this woman. Although he had no idea why he cared. She was just a stranger to him. Once he dropped her off at the inn, he probably wouldn't ever see her again.

~

FAITH LOOKED out the window at the passing storefronts all lit up for the holidays. Christmas had just passed a few weeks ago, but apparently the people of January Cove weren't in a hurry to take down their decorations.

She thought of her father and how he'd always hired a company to put up and take down their extensive holiday decorations. She hadn't exactly had the typical upbringing, but it had been hers. And now those memories felt strange to her.

It dawned on her that she was now riding in a vehicle with a man she barely knew to a place that she didn't know at all in a city she had never visited. At night. And her cell phone was dead. This was how horror movies started.

"Here we are," Brandon said as he pulled into a driveway.

"Where is here?"

"Actually, this is my house."

Faith was surprised. The house was more like a cottage with dormer windows upstairs, but it sat right on the beach. She could hear the waves crashing into the shore even before he opened her door.

"Your house? I think you might have the wrong impression..." Now she really was getting a little nervous.

"It's okay, Faith. I wasn't thinking anything like that. Can you just try to trust me?"

At this point she was so hungry and tired that she didn't even care about the outcome. Brandon walked around and opened her door after grabbing a large paper bag from behind his seat.

She followed him down a cobblestone walkway

beside the house until they were on the beach. Even at nighttime, she could see the white caps as they raced toward the sand. The moon was reflecting off the water and looked like a million little diamonds shining brightly for miles.

For a moment, she wondered what it would be like to be here with someone she loved. Her recent breakup hadn't really resulted in heartbreak, but it did make her feel like her life had been set back by years. She was no closer to getting married and having a house on the beach herself. Instead, she found herself literally starting over from scratch, trying to retrace her life from birth.

"Here we go," Brandon said as they turned the corner to reveal a small sitting area with a fire pit in the center just behind his house.

Faith walked to one of the well weathered chairs and sat down as Brandon lit the fire pit and sat down with the bag in his lap.

"It's nice out here," Faith said.

"Thanks. Not exactly a fancy restaurant, but hopefully it will do," he said smiling. He had dimples, and that made her get shivers that didn't have anything to do with cool ocean breeze currently blowing through her hair. "So I wasn't exactly sure what you like to eat, but I took some wild guesses at the grocery store," he said, handing her some kind of sandwich. He put a large fruit tray on the table between the chairs and poured some sparkling water into two paper cups.

Faith opened the sandwich, surprised to see that it was totally vegan and exactly the way she would've ordered it herself.

"Is that okay?"

Faith smiled and then felt a wave of guilt wash over her. "It's perfect. This was very sweet of you. Especially in light of how horribly I've treated you today."

"Hey, I'm the one that let the mutt run you down like a tractor trailer truck," Brandon said with a laugh as he pulled out his own sandwich.

"It was just a tough day," she said quietly. "So thanks... for this."

They sat together and ate without a lot of words between them. Faith was having a hard time keeping her eyes open, and the sound of the waves wasn't helping her elude the comatose state she was sure to be in once her head hit the pillow.

"You look exhausted."

Faith laughed. "I'm beyond exhausted. I don't even think there's a word for it. I should probably get to Addy's before it gets too late."

"Of course," Brandon said, standing up and gathering their leftover trash.

"Isn't it just down the street? I can totally walk that far."

Brandon looked at her like she'd grown a second

head. "Now, Faith McLemore, I think you know me at least well enough to know that I would never let a woman, especially an injured one, walk home in the dark."

Faith nodded. Truthfully, she was way too tired to walk to the inn anyway.

As he drove her down the street, she realized he hadn't really asked her *why* she was in January Cove, and for that she was thankful. She had no idea what she was going to say when people asked her that question.

"Oh, my father stole money from his company and the government of this great country of ours. So he's currently eating slop in prison, and I've lost everything I own. Oh, and my boyfriend left me because I'm not rich anymore, and everyone thinks I'm guilty by association. And it turns out I'm also an orphan, so I'm just here in town with little to no information looking for my long lost mother. So, yeah, I'm totally normal."

"Here we are," Brandon said, knocking Faith out of the pretend conversation in her head. The inn was beautiful at night with leftover Christmas lights still glimmering on the porch. Faith had always loved Christmas, but this year had been lonely to say the least. She'd spent it eating Chinese takeout in her tiny apartment by herself. No gift buying for anyone else, so she bought herself four entrees and binge ate all of it over the span of a few hours while watching sappy Christmas movies on TV.

41

Now it was after the first of the new year, and here she sat in a brand new place. She wanted to think about how full of possibilities it was, but really she just felt lost. And alone.

"Thanks for the ride."

Brandon nodded. "Of course. It was the least I could do considering how I welcomed you to town."

Faith laughed. "Yes, I think I can still see some of my blood on the sidewalk over there. Next time a handshake would be sufficient."

Brandon held out his hand, a slight smile on his face. "Hi. Welcome to January Cove. I'm Brandon. And you are?"

Faith slowly reached out her hand and slid it into his. There was a warmth there she hadn't expected on such a cool evening.

"Faith."

"Faith. I like that."

She could feel her face flushing and prayed that the darkened vehicle wouldn't give her away. Suddenly, she had a need to get out of the SUV and fast.

"Good night, Brandon," she said softly without making eye contact again.

"Let me walk you to the door," Brandon said, starting to open his door. Faith stopped him.

"Look, I appreciate everything you did today. I really do. But I'm not looking for anything more than acquaintances in this town. I won't be here long."

His eyebrows pulled together. "Faith, I wasn't trying to date you. This is the South, and I'm a gentleman. My Mom raised me right. I just wanted to walk you to the door."

She wasn't sure if the nervousness she felt in her stomach was from making a mistake in thinking he was trying to woo her, or if it was disappointment that he wasn't trying to impress her.

"No need. Thanks again," she said before she hobbled up the stairs and into the inn without looking back.

FAITH HADN'T SLEPT this well in a long time. She slowly opened her eyes, and it took her a moment to remember where she was. She certainly wasn't in her old bedroom, the one with the elevated four poster bed and expensive down comforter set.

Instead, she was in a bed that was made of logs with an intricate patchwork quilt keeping her warm. And it wasn't as bad as she thought it'd be.

Truthfully, when Addy had shown her the room last night, she'd wondered why anyone would ever want to stay in such a place. Each room was decorated differently, and she apparently had the "cabin themed" room. Faith had never been a cabin person.

The most rustic place she'd stayed was a hotel that didn't have an indoor pool.

Easing herself up, she rested her back against the headboard. Her head was still a little sore, and her knee felt raw but other than that, she felt well rested.

She looked at her phone, as she did every morning. No text messages. She didn't even know who she was hoping to hear from. It wasn't like her father could text her, and apparently he wanted nothing more to do with her anyway.

Faith tossed her phone on the table, slid back down under the covers and pulled the quilt over her head.

"Knock knock!" she heard Addy say while she simultaneously knocked on the thick wood door. Faith sighed.

She stood up and pulled on her robe before opening the door to see Addy standing there with a plate full of something covered by a silver dome.

"Breakfast," Addy said with a big smile as she walked past Faith into the room. "I've got coffee or fresh squeezed orange juice. Which would you like?"

"Um, coffee, I guess," Faith said.

"Great! I'll bring up a fresh cup in a quick second," Addy said, trotting off into the still darkened hallway. "Cream and sugar?" she called back over her shoulder.

"Just sugar please," Faith responded as she pulled out the chair to the small desk near her bed and took the top off the plate. On it was a stack of French toast topped with blueberries and whipped cream. The aroma was almost overwhelming.

"Here you go," Addy said, arriving back in the room at an alarming speed. Faith wondered how she had so much energy in the morning and how she managed to get back so fast without spilling the coffee on herself and everything in between.

"These look really good, but I don't think I can eat them."

"Nonsense! Enjoy yourself!"

Faith smiled. "No, I mean... I'm vegan."

Addy's face fell. "Oh my goodness. I'm so sorry, Faith. I didn't mean to offend. I just knew you had a hard day yesterday. You know, comfort food is a Southern thing."

Faith laughed. "I appreciate the sentiment. Maybe you have some fruit and oatmeal?"

"Of course. My sweetie will eat this stack in no time flat," Addy said.

"Listen, please don't put yourself out. I'll get ready and come down to the kitchen to grab something before I leave."

Addy nodded. "I don't mean to pry, Faith, but I have to ask why you're in January Cove? I mean, most of my guests are here visiting family or on business or vacation, but you don't seem to fit any of those categories."

Faith knew she'd get questions, but it was still a

bit early in the morning to answer them. Besides, the last thing she wanted was for anyone to know about her past.

"I have family here," Faith said without thinking.

"Oh really? Who? I've lived here my whole life, so I probably know them!" Addy said excitedly.

Faith froze. "Um, I…"

"Good morning, ladies," a voice said from the doorway. It was Brandon. He was holding a brown paper bag again.

"Good morning," Faith said smiling, grateful that he'd interrupted their conversation.

"Hey, Brandon," Addy said. "French toast?" She held up the plate and Brandon laughed.

"You didn't know she was vegan, did you?"

Addy looked at Faith and chuckled. "No, but I do now, so I'm going to do a little digging around on the Internet for some recipes."

"Oh, Addy, really… Please don't inconvenience yourself. I'll just go to the grocery store."

"Not an inconvenience, Faith," Addy said as she made her way to the door. "It's just part of what I do as an inn owner. It's my responsibility to make January Cove feel like home."

For some reason, that tugged on Faith's heart-strings. No one had cared about her feelings in a long time, and in less than twenty four hours, she felt like January Cove was a possible home. At least temporarily.

After Addy left the room, Brandon stood there quietly for a few moments, a thick air of awkwardness between them.

"Here," he said, handing her the bag.

Faith took it, unsure of what it could be. She looked inside and saw a couple of large muffins, one blueberry and one chocolate.

"But these can't be…"

"Vegan? Yes they are. I promise."

"You bought these for me? In January Cove?"

"Yes, I bought them for you. In January Cove? No. There's a great place near Savannah."

"Savannah? But that's more than an hour away, isn't it?"

"Depends on how fast you drive," Brandon said. "I just knew you'd need breakfast, and we got back too late last night to warn Addy, so…"

Before Faith could stop it, her eyes teared up. "Thank you."

Brandon looked at her quizzically. "Faith, it's just muffins. Are you okay?"

She laughed and wiped away a stray tear that rolled down her cheek. "I'm fine. I guess I'm just worn out from traveling and everything that's happened in the last twenty four hours."

He paused and looked at her for a moment. "Okay. If you need to talk…"

Faith held up her hand. "No. I definitely don't need to talk. But thanks for the offer."

Brandon nodded. "Well, I've got a shift at the hospital, so I'd better get going. Enjoy the muffins."

He turned to leave. "Hey, Brandon?"

"Yeah?"

"Where would I find the library around here?"

"Wow, that sounds like a fun place to hang out. You know we have a beach and a movie theater, right?"

Faith rolled her eyes. "I like to read. What can I say?"

"The library is down the road to the East, just past the high school. Not more than a mile from here, I'd say. If you need a ride, I'm heading that way."

"No thanks. I still have some things to do around here first. You know, unpack and all that." She was totally lying, but she didn't want to be in the car with him again right now. Too many questions that she didn't feel like answering.

"Okay. Well, enjoy your reading," Brandon said with a chuckle before walking out. She shut her door and walked to the window, the paper bag still dangling from her hand. She peeked through the wooden plantation shutters and watched him drive off in his SUV before taking one of the muffins from the warmth of brown paper and smiling.

CHAPTER 4

*B*randon couldn't get her out of his head, and he had no idea why. This woman wasn't his type at all. She was uptight and secretive and flew off the handle at a moment's notice.

And yet he wanted to get to know her better.

He'd driven almost to Savannah for muffins. The thought astonished even him.

"Did you release Mrs. Smith in room three?" the nurse asked him as he stared at his tablet in a haze.

"What?"

"Mrs. Smith? The woman who had the reaction to the shampoo?"

"Oh. Right. Yes, I released her. She was stable and will be following up with her doctor about getting allergy testing."

"Are you okay? You seem a little distracted today," the nurse said. There was nothing good about being labeled as distracted in the emergency room.

"I'm fine," Brandon said with a smile. "Just didn't get much sleep last night."

The nurse eyed him carefully. "Okay. Who is she?"

"Excuse me?"

"Dr. James, I've known you, what, like six years now? I've never seen you look so lovelorn."

"Lovelorn? Impossible since I'm not in love with anyone at the moment," he said, although she wasn't far off the mark. He definitely felt something... although he wasn't sure what to call it.

Brandon didn't want to fall in love. It hadn't worked out well for him in the past. In fact, he seemed attracted to women who needed "saving", and once the saving part was done, they moved on to greener pastures. At least that was how he saw it.

"Who's my next patient?" Brandon asked without moving the conversation further.

The nurse smiled and looked down at her tablet. "Room two. Possible broken wrist."

Brandon pulled the sheet back to enter the room and was surprised to see his friend, Clay sitting there.

"Hey, man! What happened?"

Clay was sitting on the table, his wrist pulled tight to his chest and a look of pain obvious on his face.

"The ferry was tied up, or so I thought. Got my hand caught between the boat and the dock."

"Ouch," Brandon said as he started to press lightly on different areas of his wrist. Clay immediately jumped in pain.

Clay had run the ferry service for a long time now, so getting hurt wasn't a typical thing for him.

"I think we'd better get this x-rayed."

Clay nodded. "Addy is going to kill me. I wasn't supposed to work the ferry today, but my guy called in sick."

"I'm sure she'll forgive you when she sees you're in pain."

"Maybe, but I have to help with the redecorating. We just bought some stuff to redo a few of the rooms we didn't get to when the place opened. I guess I'll have to help her one-handed."

"First things first," Brandon said. "I'll call for x-ray and then we'll see what we need to do from here, okay?"

～

FAITH SAT at the table in the small coffee shop she'd found near the beach. Jolt seemed to be a popular place, so it had taken her a few minutes to get a table, but now that she had one she wasn't moving for awhile.

Although the January Cove library had been

smaller than anticipated, she had been able to print off some potentially useful information including newspaper birth announcements from around the time she was born.

The thing was, she had no idea where she was really born. Her birth certificate could've been faked, or so she assumed. Since Jim wasn't answering her calls and refusing to see her, she had little information to go on other than the name of January Cove.

As she drank her latte, she scoured each item she had copied, but nothing was turning up. She sighed and crumpled up the last piece of useless paper.

"Dang it," she said to herself.

"Everything okay?" the red-haired woman behind the counter asked. The customers had finally thinned out once the lunch rush passed, and now Faith found herself alone with the woman aside from another table with an elderly gentleman.

"I'm fine," Faith said. "Sorry if I said that a little too loudly."

"No, problem at all. I'm Rebecca. You must be new in town?"

Faith chuckled. "It's hard to be incognito here, isn't it?"

Rebecca smiled. "Small towns are that way, I guess."

"I'm Faith. And yes, I'm visiting from Virginia. Staying at Addy's."

"That's wonderful. Addy's basically my sister-in-law. I date her brother, Jackson."

"Everyone really does know everyone in this town," Faith said. "It's kind of... nice."

She was surprised to hear herself say those words. Faith had never thought about living in a small town. Big city life had always been her dream. Parties, art gallery openings, wine tastings. But January Cove was different, and nothing seemed to be "missing" about it.

"So are you here for business?" Rebecca asked. Why did everyone here need to know why she was here? It was like they were protective of their town.

Faith was already getting tired of keeping up the facade. "No. I'm actually here doing a little genealogical research on my family."

Rebecca cocked her head in confusion. "You came all the way from Virginia for that? Seems the computer might have been faster... and cheaper?"

"Maybe so. But I needed a little mini vacation, so I decided to pack them into one big trip."

Rebecca smiled. "Well, be careful because January Cove has a way of reeling you in and never letting you go."

She walked away to speak to her other customer, and Faith wondered if that was true. Already, the little town was growing on her. Not that she had any plans to move there, but she could see the attraction.

It was the perfect place to start over and build a totally different life.

"We have to stop meeting like this."

She looked up to see Brandon standing there. He was wearing green scrubs, and for some reason that made her feel a little giddy inside.

"Do you ever work?" she asked with a laugh.

"I'll have you know I've been at work for four whole hours now." He put his hands on the back of the chair across from her and leaned in. "Don't tell anyone, but there's a lull in the ER right now so I came out to get coffee. Shhh...."

Faith smiled. He was cute in an irritating sort of way. "Well, don't let me interrupt you."

"I have a few minutes," he said, pulling out the chair and sitting down.

"Feel free to sit down."

Brandon grinned. "Hey, Rebecca, can I get a couple of mocha lattes for Sarah and Paul, and a black coffee for me?"

Rebecca waved and nodded as she turned around to start working on the caffeine boosts.

"So how was the library?"

"Not overly helpful."

"You know, I went to college. Maybe I can help?"

"Do you ever say anything that's not sarcastic?" she asked.

"Occasionally."

"Anyway, no there's nothing you can help with.

I'm not even sure why I'm in January Cove, to be honest."

"Faith, as far as I can tell, we're friends."

"I wouldn't go that far."

"I brought you muffins!"

She giggled. "And they were amazing. But friendship takes time to build. But we're acquaintances for sure."

"Wow, that's great. I've always wanted more acquaintances."

"Sarcasm again?"

"Look, I don't know what happened to you recently, but you've got this enormous wall up. I don't know if you could make a friend if you tried right now."

Faith's mouth dropped open. "That was harsh."

"But true, right?"

She sat there with her lips pursed for a moment. "Probably."

"And I know you have some reason why you don't trust people. But what do you really have to lose here? I mean, you could leave here and go back to Virginia anytime, right?"

"Right."

"So why not try to trust someone and see if they can help you?"

"I never said I needed any help."

"Hey, Brandon, doesn't Sarah like a shot of

vanilla in hers?" Rebecca called from behind the counter. Brandon nodded.

"It's obvious you need help. You're here in a strange town all alone. You're being very tight lipped about why you're here. People all over town are talking..."

"Seriously?" Faith asked, her mouth gaping open yet again.

"Well, no. Not yet. But they will be. That's a small town for you."

Faith took a deep breath of relief. "Look, I don't think I can get the answers I need here anyway. This trip was a rash decision I made in a moment of grief and frustration. I've been thinking about heading back to Virginia."

"Don't," he said, reaching across the table and putting his hand over hers. Faith let it sit for a beat, but then slid her hand from underneath his.

"Why?"

"I believe in gut feelings, Faith. And your gut brought you to January Cove. Now, I don't know why you're hiding so much, but I'd like to be that friend... er, acquaintance... to help you get what you need to move forward in your life."

"Why do you care so much, Brandon? You hardly know me."

He sighed. "I'm a doctor, Faith. I care about people. It's just who I am."

She stared at him for a moment. He really did

seem to be one of the most genuine people she'd ever met.

"Here you go! I put it on your tab," Rebecca said with a wink as she put the drink carrier on the table. Sensing she was interrupting a conversation, she quickly made herself scarce.

"Okay, fine."

"Fine? So you'll let me help?"

"Since you seem to have a superhero complex, I'll tell you *some* of my story," Faith said.

Brandon smiled broadly. "Great. I get off at six tonight. What do you say to a nice dinner?"

"Somewhere fancy?"

"At my house."

"I don't know…"

"Faith, I assumed you wanted privacy since you don't want the whole town knowing your business?"

He was right. "Okay. I'll be there at seven."

"I can pick you up."

"No. I'll drive myself."

Brandon looked like he wanted to argue, but knew he was on shaky ground as it was.

"Looking forward to it," he said with a wink before picking up the carrier and walking out. He waved one more time through the large plate glass window.

"That Brandon is something else, huh?" Rebecca said as she brought Faith a refill.

"Yeah, he seems to be. Are all small town doctors like him?"

Rebecca cocked her head. "Oh, sweetie, Brandon hadn't lived here in years until recently. He spent the last five years doing missionary work as a doctor in the Middle East. The man spent that time in war zones serving some of the most forgotten people on the planet. He's a true hero, that one."

Rebecca walked back to the counter, and Faith was left to wonder if she'd been misjudging Brandon all along.

~

BRANDON LOOKED AT HIS WATCH. His shift was ending soon, but he still had one more patient to discharge.

"Sarah, Mrs. Lechter can go home. She needs to fill the prescription for the antibiotic and follow up with her doctor later this week." He signed off on the paperwork and handed it to his nurse before heading to the lounge.

Brandon loved being a doctor, but it had been a big adjustment coming home to January Cove after so many years away. Still, it was home, and his mother and father didn't live far away. He felt like he needed to be close now that they were getting older.

"Headed out, Brandon?" Dr. Becker asked.

"Yes. In fact, I'm cooking dinner for Faith McLemore tonight."

Dr. Becker's eyes popped open. "Really? How on Earth did you get her to agree?"

"We've actually spent a little time together. She's not all that bad. Just a little…"

"Uptight? Pretentious?"

Brandon chuckled. "Surface stuff, Don. You have to dig down to get to the good stuff, kind of like a Tootsie Pop."

"Tootsie Pops are better on the outside, actually."

"Okay, well, I can't think of another example right now. She's been through some stuff."

"Like what?"

"Well, I don't know yet. That's what I intend to find out tonight."

Dr. Becker slapped Brandon on the shoulder. "You missed your calling, young man. I think psychology would've been a great fit for you."

"Says the man who wants me to take another shift next week…" Brandon said with a smile as he headed for the door.

"But you're a dang fine ER doctor too, Brandon James…" he called out loudly.

~

FAITH PULLED up in front of Brandon's house. She'd regretted agreeing to this dinner all afternoon, but she had no way to back out since Brandon had been on duty at the hospital.

"Just step out of your comfort zone, Faith," she said to herself as she pulled into his driveway.

"Hey there!" Brandon said from the porch, a big dimply smile on his face.

Dang, he really was handsome. Even more so in the light of the emerging sunset. He was wearing a cable knit tan sweater and jeans, and Faith felt a flutter move through her chest.

"Hey," she said as she walked up to the porch. She loved his beach house. It was quaint, but very nice for a single man. It felt like a real home, and she sort of appreciated that since her home had been a bit sanitized feeling.

"Come on in," Brandon said, opening the door for her.

The inside was a lot nicer than she'd imagined. The walls were a light gray, perfectly accenting the beach that was visible from just about every angle.

There was a large wall of floor to ceiling windows facing the ocean which cast a beautiful glow into the living room and kitchen. The off white furniture, overstuffed and looking brand new, fit the beach theme perfectly without being kitschy or tacky.

It was the way she would have decorated it herself if she'd had the chance.

"Your home is lovely, Brandon. Did you hire a decorator?"

Brandon laughed. "Nope. Actually I did it myself. It's a hobby of mine."

Faith was surprised. "Interior design is your hobby?"

"Don't tell anyone, but yes. I even like building my own furniture. See that table over there?"

Faith turned to look at his kitchen table. It was a beautiful light oak with thick, heavy duty chairs. "You built that?"

"Yes. Took me months, but I finally finished it a few weeks ago. My Dad was big into carpentry when I was a kid, so I guess I just watched him a lot. Now I use his old workshop at the house I grew up in to fiddle around with projects when I get time."

"The table is amazing. A man of many talents," she said, an easy smile spreading across her face.

"Care for a glass of wine? I've got white and red, whatever you like."

"White please," Faith said, following him into the kitchen. He pointed at a barstool at the breakfast bar. "So are your parents still living?"

Brandon poured a glass for each of them and slid hers across the counter. "Yes. They've been married for forty years and live in the same house where I grew up. It's about twenty minutes from here."

"I wouldn't even know what that was like. My Mom died when I was young."

"I'm so sorry, Faith. That's tough."

She took a sip of the wine. "Yeah, it was hard being a girl and only having my Dad…" she stopped herself. It was hard to say Jim was her Dad now, not because he'd lied about her adoption but because he'd basically disowned her recently.

"Are you okay?"

She stared at her glass. "I'm fine."

"So your Dad raised you in Virginia?"

She took in a deep breath. "Yes."

"Faith, you can trust me. I won't tell anyone why you're here."

Faith smiled. "It's not like I'm here to start a drug smuggling ring or something."

"Good to know. I can cross that off my list."

"Funny. Look, I've just had a rough few months."

"When I was seventeen, I lost my older brother to a boating accident."

"I'm sorry."

"It's been a long time, but you never really get over that kind of thing, do you? I remember for the longest time after he died, I'd walk into a room and just lose it. Maybe I'd see one of his old baseball trophies or even an old sweat sock," Brandon said shaking his head. "Grief is funny that way."

Faith nodded and took a sip of her wine. "Grief comes in many forms, unfortunately, and not just after someone dies."

Brandon eyed her carefully. "Very true."

There was a moment between them where the silence seemed to speak louder than their words.

"In medical school, I took a psychology class. I did a paper that year about the effect of grief on a person's health. It's scary how much it can change a person's physiological make up, especially if the person doesn't have an appropriate outlet for their grief. You know, like talking to a trusted friend..."

"Or drinking lots of wine..." Faith said smiling before she took a long sip.

"Very funny. Why do I get the feeling that you're not much into sharing your innermost thoughts, Faith McLemore?"

"It just wasn't done in my house, I guess. My father worked a lot, so I was on my own much of the time. I mean we had house workers and so forth, but it just wasn't the same."

"House workers?"

"Oh yes. Housekeepers, a chef, a nanny..."

"Wow. Who was your father, the Duke of Virginia?"

"That's quite an education you got there, Brandon. Believe it or not, there's no Duke of Virginia," she whispered before pouring herself another glass of wine.

Brandon reached for the bottle before she could fill the glass. "Faith, we haven't had dinner yet. I'd love it if you wouldn't drink the whole bottle before

I've even had a chance to serve my famous vegan pasta dish to you."

"Wait. You cooked pasta for me? How?"

"Well, first I removed the large pot from that cabinet over there…"

"Very funny. I mean how did you have time when you just got off work an hour ago?"

"Prep is key in these situations," he said as he stood up. "Cut up the veggies this morning, made the sauce, and now all I have to do is boil the pasta."

Faith watched him fill the pot with water. "At least let me help you, Dr. James."

"Oooh, Dr. James. I like the formality. Here, you can cut open the pasta package. The scissors are in the drawer on the end," he said pointing across the kitchen.

Faith opened the drawer and retrieved the pair of scissors. She noticed a photo of Brandon with a small child, the desert landscape obvious in the background.

"That's Hassan," Brandon said.

"Rebecca told me you worked over there for a long time. Is this a boy you helped?"

Brandon smiled, but there was a hint of sadness. "I helped as much as I could. His mother had been maimed in a terrorist incident. Their village was very dangerous. Hassan had seen a lot of very bad things, and he was the head of their family at just ten years old."

Faith instinctively put her hand on her chest. "Oh my gosh, how awful. Whatever happened to him and his mother?"

Brandon leaned against he counter and took the photo from the drawer. He stared at it for a moment, the look on his face like he was a million miles away.

"His mother lost her legs. The last I heard, they were in refugee camp on the outskirts of their town. I had to leave before I could say goodbye."

Faith's eyes welled unexpectedly. She wasn't normally one for emotion, but just the look on Brandon's face made her sad. "That had to be hard."

Brandon put the photo back in the drawer and closed it. "It was very hard. There were so many people there who needed help, even just basic medical assistance, and it was impossible to help them all. It was frustrating at times. Not only were we always short on supplies and medications, but we spent a lot of time running for cover when fighting would begin."

Faith felt a tugging at her heart. Here she was fixating on her situation when people in other parts of the world had it so much worse than she ever thought about. And what had she done with her life to this point? Nothing. No volunteer work. No serving the homeless or working at an animal shelter. She'd spent her life being waited on hand and foot and shopping in the fanciest stores. It was embarrassing.

"How's that pasta coming along?" Brandon asked. Faith didn't realize she'd been standing there with the bag in one hand and the scissors in the other.

"Oh, sorry. I was just thinking."

"Yeah, it's overwhelming, isn't it? So many people who need help in this world."

Faith handed him the open bag. "Yes, but at least you've helped people. I haven't done a thing in my life to help someone."

Brandon looked at her surprised. "You've never volunteered?"

"Nope. I'm a horrible person."

"You're definitely not a horrible person, Faith. If you'd like to volunteer, I know of some great local organizations."

Faith's stomach clenched up. If she volunteered in January Cove, it meant she was staying for awhile. It was a commitment. But what else did she have to do? Of course, once her money ran out, she'd need a job but she had the gift of time right now.

"Okay, yes. I'd like to know of some places."

Brandon smiled. "Good. We can chat about it over our dinner."

CHAPTER 5

Faith couldn't remember a time when she'd laughed harder. Brandon was actually a pretty funny guy. He'd regaled her with tales from his trip to the Middle East, but also with humorous stories about growing up in January Cove.

"One time, my brother and I went over to the island and..."

"Island?"

"Oh, yeah. There are several little uninhabited islands around here, but locals here go to one of them by ferry. Just a place to chill out, maybe have a picnic or play frisbee."

"That sounds like fun," Faith said, taking the last bite of her pasta.

Brandon grinned. "Well then maybe we can go one day?"

"We'll see," she said, rolling her eyes.

"Hey, that's progress. You didn't shoot me down immediately."

"Contrary to what you might think, Brandon, I'm not always a horrible, anti-social person," she said, pointing her fork at him.

"I don't think that at all, actually."

"No?"

"I think you're a wounded person."

"Still playing psychologist?"

"Well, I can't help but remind you that tonight was supposed to be all about you sharing some of your reason for being in January Cove with me."

"I haven't forgotten," Faith said, taking a gulp of her sweet tea.

"And yet all we've talked about is the Middle East, the island and that one time I got mono in tenth grade from kissing the wrong girl."

"Still makes me laugh," Faith said.

"So what brought you to our little Southern oasis, Miss McLemore?"

Faith took a deep breath and let it out. "I'm not as good at sharing as you are."

"Okay, maybe it will help if I ask some questions."

"Whatever floats your boat."

"So I know your mother passed away when you were young. What did your father do for a living?"

"He was in finance."

"And your father is still living?"

Faith stared at Brandon for a moment. "Yes, Jim McLemore is most certainly alive."

"Okay, that was a weird way to answer the question, Faith. Almost robotic."

"Next question please."

Brandon rolled his eyes. "You realize you can be a bit exhausting, right?"

"Noted."

"Okay, next question. Where is Jim McLemore right now, Faith?"

Faith froze in her seat. A lump formed in her throat. Suddenly, she swore the room was starting to spin, so she held on to the arms of the chair she was sitting in.

"Faith, are you okay?"

She swallowed hard and took a deep breath. "I'm... I'm fine."

"No you're not. Here, drink some water," he said, sliding a bottle of water across the table. "I'm sorry if I hit a nerve. You don't have to..."

"He's in prison."

Brandon stopped and looked at her. "Oh, Faith, I'm so sorry I asked. I was just trying to..."

"It's okay. I needed to say it to somebody. My father... or Jim, rather... is in prison for embezzling money from everybody and their brother."

"That's tough. To lose your mother and now your father."

Faith laughed ironically. "Yeah."

"Am I missing something?"

"They aren't my biological parents, Brandon."

"Oh."

"And I had no idea until a couple of weeks ago when Jim... my Dad... gave me information on a safety deposit box. Inside was a letter from him and the name of this town."

"Wow, I don't even know what to say. So he never told you that you were adopted?"

"Nope. Lied to me my whole life. And when I tried to go back and see him, to ask him more questions, he refused to see me. Even sends my letters back. He's pushed me out of his life, and now I literally have no one."

Why was she telling him all this? She'd promised herself she would only give him enough information to stop him from asking so many questions. But her mouth was shooting out information faster than she could stop it.

"You're not alone, Faith," Brandon said, reaching over and covering her hand with his.

She wanted to pull her hand away, but the touch of another human seemed necessary right now. Faith hadn't realized just how alone in the world she felt until now.

"So you came here to look for your birth parents then?"

"I guess. Honestly, I don't know enough to even start looking."

"That's why you visited the library?"

"Yes. Although it was pretty pointless since I don't know anything to look up on those old microfiche machines. This town really needs to upgrade to computers."

Brandon laughed. "True story."

"So I don't know why I'm still here, racking up a bill staying with Addy, when I don't have the first clue to go on."

"Maybe because Virginia doesn't feel like home anymore?"

Faith pondered his statement for a moment. "Maybe. But nowhere feels like home anymore. I'm literally an orphan."

"Faith, you're not an orphan. As mad as you are at your Dad…"

"Jim."

"Okay, Jim. As mad as you are at Jim, he raised you. And he apparently loved you."

"How do you lie to someone you love for so many years?"

"It was wrong, Faith. I get that. But other than that, he sounds like he was a decent father to you? And you had a good mother too, right?"

"For a little while anyway."

"Do you have any other family in Virginia?"

"Not really. I'm an only child, and when my Da… Jim… did what he did, everyone basically painted a giant scarlet letter on my chest."

"It couldn't have been that bad."

"Oh no? My boyfriend of three years dumped me, my supposed best friend changed her phone number and my friends from the fancy private school I attended for twelve years of my life didn't even invite me to our reunion."

"Ouch."

"Rich people can be very mean, trust me."

Brandon suddenly laughed out loud.

"Excuse me? This is funny to you? See, this is why I don't trust people," Faith said, standing up from the table.

Brandon tried to straighten his face and grabbed Faith's arm. "No, you don't understand."

"You're literally trying not to laugh at me right now!"

"Faith, I'm laughing because I'm envisioning you trying to come here for a fresh start and the first thing that happens is a huge dog tackles you…" Brandon said before dissolving into a puddle of laughter again. This time, Faith joined him, slowly at first. But within seconds, she had tears pouring down her face. She slid back into her chair and tried to catch her breath.

"Yeah, that was quite a welcome," she said, dabbing a napkin at her eyes.

"I'm so sorry," he said laughing. "But I'm also not sorry."

"Oh really? And why is that?"

"Because it allowed me to meet you," Brandon said softly. Faith felt her insides clench up a bit. This guy was gorgeous and smart and level-headed. But right now she was in no place to have feelings for anyone, let alone the guy who had to be the most eligible bachelor in town. That would only lead to inevitable heartbreak somewhere down the line.

"Thanks," she said, breaking eye contact and picking up her plate. She carried it to the sink, Brandon not far behind.

"You're not comfortable with emotions, are you?"

"I'm comfortable with *some* emotions."

"Such as?"

"Anger," Faith said with a smile.

Brandon touched her arm. "Faith, there's a lot more you have to give inside that big heart of yours."

"Maybe I don't have a big heart."

"I'm a good judge of people, and I know you have so much to offer this world. You're just raw right now. You've been hurt in so many ways. I get it. But don't shut people out. Don't shut me out. I want to help you, so just let me, okay?"

God, he was hard to resist. Right now she wanted to grab his face and kiss him, so she balled her fists up by her sides and dug her fingernails into the palms of her hands.

"Thanks, Brandon. But I really don't know how you can help me."

Brandon stepped back and crossed his arms, a

thoughtful look on his face. "Well, for one thing I can hook you up with a great volunteer opportunity."

"Tell me more."

"There's an amazing new organization here called HOPE. They provide backpacks for food insecure youth in our surrounding areas."

"Food insecure?"

"There are hundreds of kids in our local schools who don't have food unless they're at school. So over weekends, holidays and the summer break, these kids may not eat."

Faith stared at him. "You're serious?"

"You've never heard this?" Brandon asked, his eyes widened.

Faith shook her head. "Never. I told you. I'm a horrible person."

"You're not horrible, Faith. You just weren't informed. How do you feel hearing this?"

She thought for a moment. "Terrible. That must be awful for these kids. I just can't imagine not knowing where my next meal will come from."

Brandon smiled and playfully punched her arm. "See? You have a big heart in there, and we're going to put it to good use. I'll hook you up with Olivia. She runs the organization, and I'm sure she can find something you'll be great at."

For the first time in a long time, Faith felt like she had something to look forward to. Even if she couldn't help herself, maybe by helping others she would find a purpose for her trip to January Cove.

∼

BRANDON SAT ON HIS DECK, staring out into the vast expanse of the ocean. He loved this view. It never got old. Five years in the desert had made him appreciate it all the more. But still, he worried for those people he left behind. Talking about it with Faith had brought up so many emotions. Sometimes he even considered going back because there were days in January Cove where he felt he wasn't helping enough people.

His mother had always said Brandon's heart was bigger than his brain at times. He acted without thinking anytime someone needed help, even in relationships. His past was a scattered mess of break ups with women who couldn't seem to understand his need to help others. He'd had a history of trying to "fix" broken women too, and that had led to many nights of staring at the same expanse of water, trying to figure out if God had a woman out there just for him.

He couldn't help but think about his dinner with Faith last night. She was a hard one to figure out. On the one hand, they were nothing alike. She came from such vast amounts of wealth that he had a hard time imagining what her formative years were like.

She'd had real English tea parties at her house while he'd eaten pineapple and mayonnaise sandwiches as a treat after school. She'd had a nanny that attended to her every need while he'd had a babysitter that spent most of her time outside smoking instead of watching him. She'd had a brand new red sports car at sixteen years old. He'd ridden his bicycle to school, and it didn't have working brakes so he'd worn out the bottoms of his sneakers trying to stop.

Brandon had had to work for everything in his life. His parents were good, hard working people, but they'd never had a lot of money. Doing well in school and getting scholarships resulted in him being the first college educated person in his family.

But there was more to Faith than met the eye. He could see through her strong, standoffish persona. Inside, she was scared. She was vulnerable. She was aching for something more.

He knew what that felt like. And, against all of his better judgment, he was going to help her get back on her feet, even if it meant fighting every instinct he had to scoop her up into his arms and protect her from the world.

~

FAITH SAT in the small waiting room, tapping her foot on the freshly carpeted floor as anxiety continued to course around her body. Brandon had set up this appointment for her to meet Olivia, but she was starting to second guess the whole thing.

After all, what did she know about kids and poverty? Exactly nothing. She wouldn't have anything to offer these children, and they'd sense that. Kids and dogs can always sense when you don't know what you're doing, right?

"You must be Faith?" a woman said from the doorway. She was very attractive with platinum blond hair, perfect for the beach. She looked to be in her mid thirties, maybe, and seemed like a poster model for the quaint coastal town.

"Yes, that's me," Faith said, summoning her best smile without looking like a nutcase. She stood up and shook the woman's hand.

"Hi. I'm Olivia Lane. Welcome to HOPE!"

"Thanks for meeting with me."

"Come on back to my office," Olivia said, opening the door wider.

Faith followed her to a small office off of a bigger room that looked to be used for events.

"Sorry about the mess. We're still getting moved into this place. I ran HOPE out of my home for months until my husband threatened to run away," she said with a laugh. "Have a seat."

Faith sat down in a chair across from her desk. "It's a nice place." She had no idea what to say.

"Brandon tells me that you might want to volunteer while you're visiting January Cove?"

"I'm definitely interested in doing that, yes. But I've never volunteered anywhere before so I don't know how much help I'd be, honestly."

"Oh, honey, trust me, we can use an extra pair of hands every single day!"

"Really?"

"Absolutely. For example, the kids just got back to school after winter break so now we're trying to get more donations for spring break backpacks."

"Spring break backpacks?"

"Yes. We send home fully stocked backpacks so that our food insecure kids have plenty to eat during spring break."

Faith's stomach tightened. "So there really are kids who wouldn't have food if they weren't in school?" Part of her hadn't believed Brandon when he told her.

"Yes, that's very true. We have kids who only get food at school."

"That makes me so sad." Faith really did feel sad. Maybe Brandon was right and she did have a big heart in there.

"Around here, we turn our sadness into HOPE," she said, smiling as she pointed behind her at their slogan on the wall. "Sadness is a useless emotion without action. I've been through a few rough spots in my life, and there were people who helped me.

So, I consider it my job and my duty to help others."

"That's very inspiring."

"Care to join us?" Olivia asked, her hands in a prayer position.

Faith smiled. "I'd love to."

And with that, Faith McLemore put down some roots in January Cove.

~

"So, HOW WAS YOUR FIRST DAY?" Brandon asked as he took a bite of his sandwich. He'd been surprised when Faith had invited him to eat a quick lunch at the sandwich place near the pier. She was getting easier to be around as her walls started to come down a bit.

"I was a mess this morning. I've never really been around kids, but we had an event at the elementary school."

"Oh yeah? What did you do?"

"I colored with some third graders. I played a little dodge ball with some aggressive fourth graders. And I ate lunch with this sweetest little girl named Sadie. Well, not alone. Olivia sat with us. I just listened mostly."

"Sadie, huh?" Brandon couldn't help but smile at her excitement.

"She was pretty adorable, actually. Curly black

hair and the biggest smile. Olivia told me that her parents divorced and she's being raised right now by her great aunt. But money is tight, so Sadie gets most of her meals through the school and HOPE."

"Wow."

"Yeah, it's crazy to think there are kids all around this country who go to bed hungry. I guess I never really thought about it, but now I won't ever forget it. Putting faces to the issue makes it even more important to me."

"And that's just after one day, Faith. Amazing!"

Faith smiled at him. "I wanted to say thanks for introducing me to Olivia."

"No problem at all."

"And thanks for making me believe I had something to give."

Brandon looked at her. "You have a lot to give, Faith. Stop doubting yourself."

"Hard habit to break," she said, biting into a French fry.

"I've always found that during the worst times of our lives, the best thing to do is help someone else. There are always people worse off than you are."

"So what has been the worst time of your life, Brandon?"

He sighed. "I was left at the altar."

Faith's face changed. He couldn't figure out if it was shock or some form of anger, but it did cause her to drop her sandwich.

"What?"

"Yep. It was almost six years ago now."

"What kind of idiot woman would leave you at the altar?" she said, obviously without thinking. Her eyes popped open wider, and he could see her face starting to turn red.

"Her name was Kim. We dated a couple of years, planned a big wedding and then when the big day arrived, she didn't."

"Did you ever talk to her again?"

"On the phone. Eventually my mom found out she was hiding in another state with her aunt and uncle. She just didn't know how to tell me that she didn't want to go through with it, I guess. So she ran. Her bridesmaids didn't even know. They walked down the aisle and she ran out the back door of the church and hopped a bus to Indiana."

Faith stared at him like he was an alien. "That's the most depressing and entertaining story I've ever heard."

Brandon laughed. "Well, it wasn't entertaining at the time."

"I'm so sorry that happened to you, Brandon. You definitely deserve so much better."

He held her gaze for a moment and felt something deep in his soul. What if she was "the one"? *No. No. No. Stop it, Brandon, he thought to himself. She's just as wounded as you are, if not more.*

"Well, anyway, that's how I ended up overseas. I

had to get out of here and away from all the memories… the embarrassment…"

"So you used your pain to help others."

"Right. And that's what I think you should do. It changes who you are because you realize what's really important."

"And what did you realize?"

"That my purpose on this Earth is to help other people survive. And that the only thing that matters… the only thing that really lasts… is love."

Faith swallowed hard. "Do you regret not getting married?"

Brandon paused for a moment. "Absolutely… not."

"Really?"

"Looking back, she was never the right one. Sometimes God just has to let you go through things to grow."

Faith nodded. "You're an old soul, Brandon James."

CHAPTER 6

F aith sat at the small desk in her room at Addy's and stared at the paper in her hands. Why had her father left her so little information? Did he know more?

Of course, she had no way to ask him. All of her letters had been returned to her, and no matter how many times she called the prison, they wouldn't help her. He'd phased her out of his life.

She had searched the Internet, visited the January Cove library and looked at every face in town just trying to see if anyone looked like her. Nothing seemed to add up.

But her visit to January Cove hadn't been in vain. After all, she'd met a great friend in Brandon, and she was starting to get a lot closer to Addy and Olivia. She loved her new "job" of volunteering too.

Life was definitely better when no one knew her past. Well, except Brandon.

Brandon was the least judgmental person she'd ever met. He had nothing but acceptance for everyone, and she wanted to be more like him. And the truth was, she was very attracted to him. The thought scared her. The last time she trusted men, she got dumped by one and abandoned by another.

"Knock knock," Addy said from the cracked doorway.

"Oh, hey, Addy," Faith said, sliding the piece of paper under her desk calendar.

"I was wondering if you were busy today?"

"Nope, not at all. Did you need some help around here?"

Addy laughed. "No. I wanted to invite you to our big Sunday family dinner."

"Family dinner?"

"All of the Parkers get together on Sundays and eat a big meal together at my Mom's house. She's traveling with her husband, but all of my brothers and their families will be there."

"I'd hate to intrude."

"Honey, I wouldn't invite you if it was an intrusion! Look, we're a very laid back, welcoming bunch. I regularly invite my guests to come."

"Oh. Well, okay then. I'd love to!"

"Great. We'll be leaving around noon, so you can just meet us in the foyer."

Faith nodded as Addy closed the door behind her. She was nervous about meeting more new people and possibly getting asked questions she didn't want to answer.

~

"AND THIS IS my brother Jackson. I think you know Rebecca already?" Addy asked as she continued introducing Faith to her large family.

"I do. She makes a mean mocha latte," Faith said with a smile.

So far, it wasn't so bad. Her mind had led her to believe that people were going to bombard her with a million questions the moment she walked through the door of the Parker home, but nothing could've been further from the truth. Instead, she had been greeted with smiles and hugs and the smell of pot roast.

A part of her longed for the camaraderie of siblings and a big family. The warmth of this over-sized family unit was something she wanted for herself. She'd grown up wealthy, but lonely, and she would've traded all the nannies and sports cars in the world for this. The feeling that someone had her back no matter what. The embrace of people who loved her and would never let her down.

"So Addy tells me you're volunteering with Olivia Lane?" Jackson said.

"Yes. I just started."

"Olivia's a great lady. We went to high school together, actually."

"Really?"

"She had a bit of a rough upbringing, but she's definitely using that to the advantage of kids all over this area."

Faith listened as he went on about the work HOPE was doing in the community, but in the back of her mind she had to wonder about the rough upbringing comment. Olivia hadn't really talked about her early years, of course why would she? Faith was a virtual stranger.

"Sorry I'm late!" she heard a voice call from the foyer. She turned around to see Brandon hugging Addy in the doorway of the kitchen.

"Brandon?"

"Oh, hey, Faith! I see Addy has wrangled you into a Parker family dinner, huh?"

She was actually happy to see a familiar face. "Didn't take much wrangling, actually. Kind of getting tired of eating alone in my room," Faith said.

"Now, I always invite you down for every meal, Faith McLemore," Addy chided.

"I know, I know. I just hate to have you dirty up the kitchen for just me."

Addy forced a frown. "Business has been a bit slow, but the busy season is almost upon us!"

The rest of the afternoon was spent laughing and

talking around the big dining room table, extra chairs spilling out from the edges. Faith couldn't remember a time where she felt more included and at peace. No one was judging her, at least that she could tell. They seemed to want to know her, not her past.

The relationships she saw around her gave her hope that one day she'd find someone who loved her for her. Only right now, she didn't really know who she was. Or where she came from.

"Thanks again, everyone. Lunch was amazing," Faith said as she made her way to the door. Addy had asked her if she wanted a ride back to the inn, but Faith had said she was going to take a nice walk along the beach first.

"Mind if I tag along?" Brandon whispered in her ear at the door. The warmth of his breath on her neck gave her shivers.

"Sure."

They made their way down through the path leading to the beach. It was starting to get cool as the evening air descended and the wind coming off the water blew her carefully styled hair all over the place. Faith pulled her cardigan tighter around her.

"So what'd you think?"

"About what? The Parker family?"

"Yes. Our resident royal family, so to speak," Brandon said with a laugh.

"They're fantastic. I wish…"

"You wish what?"

"That I had a family like that," she said as she stared back up at the towering brick house off in the distance.

"Everyone does. The Parker family is a dying breed."

"Well, that sounds morbid, Brandon."

"No, I just mean family sizes are getting smaller, and people don't stay together like they have. They've all come back to January Cove over the years, for different reasons, but they stay together by choice."

"I can't even get my father to talk to me, so I don't think I have much hope of having a family like that."

Brandon stopped and stared out toward the water as the sky began to turn pink in preparation for the impending sunset. "You see that out there?"

"What? The horizon?" Faith asked.

"Yeah. A lot of times I look at that and it reminds me that life, and all the possibilities that it brings, is limitless. You never know what's going to happen, Faith. You create what you want in this world." He turned back to her. "If you want that kind of family, you have to make it yourself."

"I don't even have a boyfriend, Brandon," she said with a laugh.

"Then maybe you should start there," he said with a wink. She had no idea what that meant, and she was far too scared to ask so she started walking again instead.

"I can't believe this place is real."

"What?"

"It's like January Cove is trapped in some time warp where people love each other and welcome strangers and the views are the most beautiful I've ever seen."

"Tell me about it," Brandon said under his breath. She turned to notice him looking at her, and her face flushed. Brandon cleared his throat. "So, do you like dolphins?"

"What?"

He cleared his throat again. "Do you like dolphins?"

"I think so... Why?"

"My friend runs a dolphin cruise company. I thought maybe you'd like to go on a tour sometime? See some dolphins?"

She smiled. "I'd like that."

Brandon smiled back. "Me too."

～

FAITH SAT at the small cafeteria table, her foot nervously tapping the floor.

"Faith?" Olivia said.

"Yes?"

"You know how they say dogs can smell fear?" she asked as she sat down in front of her.

"Yes."

"These kids are going to smell you from a mile away, sweetie."

"They are?"

"Or maybe they might get seasick first," she said, pointing at Faith's leg.

"Sorry," Faith said sighing. "I'm not sure I'm cut out for this, Liv. Maybe I could just work more behind the scenes."

Olivia reached out and took both of Faith's hands in hers. "You're a human being. These kids are no different than you are. They need to hear positive words. They need a smile and maybe a hug. Trust me, when they see HOPE volunteers here to eat lunch with them, they feel so important!"

Today was a big day for Faith. Once a month, some of the volunteers went to one of the local schools to have lunch with the HOPE kids. They didn't wear their normal T-shirts because Olivia said the kids might get bullied for needing free lunches. Instead, they were just there to encourage the kids and let them know someone cares. And this was the first time Faith would be eating with one of the kids by herself.

"They're going to love you, Faith. Just be yourself."

"I don't know who that is," Faith whispered

under her breath as Olivia stood to greet the kids who were milling into the cafeteria.

Faith stood and painted on a smile. "Faith, this is Amelia."

The little girl looked to be about nine or ten years old. She was wearing a plain pink shirt with a couple of small holes near the bottom and a pair of ratty blue jeans. Her hair was pulled into a matted ponytail. Faith wasn't ready for this.

"Hi, Amelia. I'm Faith."

"Yeah, I know. She just said that," the little girl said as she sat down. Olivia glanced at Faith and smiled.

"It's okay," she mouthed quietly. "Amelia, Miss Faith is going to have lunch with you today. Would that be alright?"

"I guess," Amelia said, shrugging her shoulders.

Faith slowly sat down across from the little girl. She noticed no one else was coming to their table.

"Aren't your friends going to sit with us too?" Faith finally asked as she opened her own bagged lunch.

"I don't have any friends," Amelia said nonchalantly as she pulled her sandwich from the bag provided by HOPE. The bag lunches were a special occurrence as most kids just ate lunch provided by the school.

Faith pushed the straw through her juice box.

"Oh, certainly that can't be true. I bet you have at least a few friends."

Amelia took a bite out of her sandwich like a ravenous animal and stared at Faith. "Nobody here talks to me."

"Nobody?"

"They make fun of me."

Faith looked at her and couldn't imagine the other kids making fun of such a beautiful little girl who couldn't help the situation she was in. "Why do they make fun of you?"

"Because we're poor." She continued to eat, no real emotion showing on her face. For Amelia, this was all the life she had known so far. It made Faith's stomach knot up.

"You know what?"

"What?"

"When I was a kid, I got bullied too."

That caught Amelia's attention. She opened her bag of chips and shoved a few in her mouth. "Why'd you get bullied?"

"Well, I had this big gap in my teeth. Right here," Faith said, pointing to where it had been before Dr. Gilmore had fixed it when she was in eighth grade.

"Where'd it go?"

"The dentist fixed it for me," Faith said.

"Dentist? Your parents must have been rich."

Faith felt completely inadequate in that moment.

She couldn't compare her situation to Amelia's. She was a fraud.

"Would you like the rest of my sandwich?" Faith asked after a few moments.

Amelia reached for it without answering and gobbled down the half Faith hadn't eaten. Her appetite had disappeared the more she realized how bad some of these kids had it. How could she have been so blind all these years?

When lunch was over, Faith told Amelia goodbye and watched her walk down the hall alone. It made her heart ache.

She rode back to the office with Olivia, the car ride quiet as she thought about all she'd experienced. When they finished unloading the car, Olivia called her into the small break room.

"You okay, hon?"

"Not really. That was a lot to take in."

"That little Amelia is something else, huh? She's a spitfire for sure."

"It's so sad. She said no one talks to her and some kids bully her for being poor."

Olivia nodded sadly. "That's true. We've been working with the counselors at the school to see if we can help. But it's hard because of her family situation."

"What do you mean?"

"Amelia was abandoned by her father as a baby. Her mother has a severe drug addiction, and they live either in her beat up car or at the homeless shelter when there's room. Her mother keeps failing drug screenings, so they get kicked out of the shelter a lot."

"Oh my gosh."

"It's very sad. There's talk that Child Protective Services is about to remove Amelia from her mother's care yet again, but she has no family so she'll be placed in foster care. It's happened a couple of times already."

Faith's heart sank. That poor little girl deserved a great life, and she definitely wasn't getting a fair shake. "Can I visit with her more often?"

Olivia smiled. "Of course!"

"Something about her just broke my heart," Faith said, still shaken by the short lunch visit with Amelia.

"She reminds me a lot of myself," Olivia said offhandedly.

"What do you mean?"

"Well, I had a very similar upbringing. My mother left me with my father when I was two years old. He was a raging, abusive alcoholic. I wanted to live with my aunt, but she got sick with cancer and couldn't take me. I ended up running away when I was thirteen, but got picked up by the police over near Savannah. They placed me with three foster families over the years, but nobody could tame me. I was a wild child, for sure. I eventually aged out of foster care."

"Wow. It's amazing you are doing so well in your life now."

"I owe a lot of that to January Cove. My last foster family lived on the edge of town. They were horrible people, unfortunately, but being here allowed me to go to January Cove High School. When I started school here, I was a mess. Still running away, but those teachers and the friends I met here were my saving grace."

"So that's why you started HOPE?"

"Yes. I know firsthand what it's like to feel unwanted and invisible. Giving back helps me. Every time I help a kid, it chips away at the hurts I have from my own past."

"But look at you now. Married and happy and running this wonderful charity. Do you and your husband have kids?"

Olivia smiled sadly. "No. We tried for years, but it wasn't in the cards for us."

"There's still time," Faith said, trying to encourage her.

"Actually, no there's not. I had to have a hysterectomy when I was thirty-two. But it's okay. I think of these kids as my own. God always has a plan."

Faith was astounded at her... well, faith. She was almost embarrassed to think she had any real problems compared to what she was seeing. Her eyes were finally wide open, and as mad as she was at her father, she knew nothing about true tough times.

"I'm so sorry."

"Oh, sweetie, it's fine. I've had eight years to grieve that loss, and I'm okay. Really."

"Wait. Eight years? You're forty years old?"

Olivia laughed. "Yes... Actually, almost forty-one."

"Oh wow. You don't look a day over thirty-five."

"Thanks. Probably because I don't have kids!" she said with a laugh. Faith couldn't help but chuckle at that too. "Come on, we have work to do."

CHAPTER 7

F aith picked at her sandwich, staring out at the ocean instead of filling her growling stomach. She'd volunteered all morning and forgot to eat breakfast, so she should've been gobbling up everything in sight right now. Instead, she was lost in thought about Amelia.

"Is something wrong with your sandwich, sweetie?" the waitress asked as she passed by to refill her sweet tea.

"Oh, no. It's great. Just have a lot on my mind."

The waitress eyed her for a moment longer and smiled. "Well, that water out there always soothes my weary soul. I'm sure it'll do the same for you, honey."

Faith nodded and smiled as the woman moved to the next table. She didn't know why Amelia's plight was bothering her so much, but she'd barely slept last night thinking about her. That tiny little freckled covered face hid so many hurts.

"Penny for your thoughts?"

Faith turned to see Brandon standing there, a penny between his thumb and index fingers stretched out in front of him.

"Jeez, man, do you ever go to work?"

Brandon put the penny on the table and tugged at his scrub top. "I think this should be an obvious answer, Faith."

She laughed. "You seem to show up everywhere I am. Are you following me?"

Brandon slid into the chair across from her. "Yes. I'm a former CIA agent, but now that I've told you, I'll have to kill you."

"Can I finish my sandwich first?"

"Since I know how good their sandwiches are, I'll allow it."

Faith loved being around Brandon. He made her feel at ease and even somewhat at home. She no longer felt like a stranger in January Cove.

"You okay?" he asked.

"I guess so. Just a little overwhelmed."

Brandon slid the penny across the table. "My offer stands."

Faith picked up the penny and put it in her pocket. "I need all the money I can get."

"So what's going on?"

"There's a little girl I met yesterday. I had lunch

with her. Her situation has me rattled. I feel like I need to do something more for her, but I don't know what."

Faith spent a few moments recounting her lunch with Amelia as Brandon listened intently. When she was finished, she sighed and leaned back in her chair.

"Wow, that's a terrible situation. How can I help?"

Her heart felt like it was going to burst out of her chest. Who was this man? How was he so amazing? And why hadn't some smart woman snatched him out of bachelorhood yet?

"I wish I knew. I feel so helpless."

"Well, let's see if I can help. When I have a problem, I like to think about what successfully solving it would mean."

"I don't understand."

"Like, in a perfect world, what would you want to see happen for Amelia?"

"Well, I'd want her in a safe home full of love and food and everything she needs to be happy. I'd want her to stop getting bullied at school too."

"So how do we move her toward that goal?"

"I don't know, Brandon. That's why I'm picking my sandwich apart and staring at the water. I told you, I'm not cut out for all of this."

He smiled at her and covered her hand with his. "Yes you are. That's why this is bothering you so much, Faith. God is calling you to action on this girl's behalf."

She felt his words in the deepest part of her soul. He was right. She felt like she was here, in this moment and in this particular place, for a purpose. But she had no idea what it was.

"When I sat across from her, I felt like…" she said before stopping herself.

"Like what?"

"I don't want to say. It's stupid."

"Just say it, Faith. What did you feel like?"

She drew in a deep breath. "I felt like I was supposed to be her mother."

She swallowed hard and waited for him to react. To laugh at her. To shake his head in disbelief at her wild notion. But he just smiled and squeezed her hand.

"Then there's your answer."

"Come on, Brandon. I'm not even a resident here. I have no paying job. And I'm certainly not vetted as a foster parent. There's no chance I could adopt this little girl."

"Maybe you're right. But maybe you're wrong. Look, as a doctor, I learned a long time ago that there are many solutions to a problem if you're willing to get creative."

Faith shook her head. "I came here to get answers about my birthmother, not to become a mother myself."

"Which one feels more important to you right in this moment, Faith?"

"It doesn't matter. I have to get my head out of the clouds. This is never going to happen. I just need to focus on helping Olivia at the charity and getting back home."

Brandon cocked his head to the side. "Maybe you're already home, Faith."

～

BRANDON COULDN'T GET their conversation out of his mind as he laid in bed trying to get to sleep. Faith was the most interesting woman he'd ever met. She was a conundrum sometimes, an unsolvable equation that vexed his mind.

He tossed and turned as he thought about how to help her. She was obviously worried about the little girl she mentioned, and he wanted to help her. But wasn't this what he always did? Got involved with women who had major problems that he felt obligated to solve?

He'd promised himself that he wouldn't do it again. He wasn't going get wrapped up in drama or problems or worries or strange entanglements. He was going to focus on his work as a doctor and get back to the Middle East to help the people he left behind as soon as possible. Only he didn't want to leave her behind now either.

~

OLIVIA LIFTED the box of food onto the table and dropped it with a thud. "You wouldn't think a box of cookies would weigh so much!"

"I could've helped you," Faith said laughing.

"I know, but I'm trying to build up my muscles. My husband, Ed, wants us to do one of those crazy obstacle course things this summer. You know the ones where you crawl through mud and call it fun?"

"Yikes! That sounds…scary?"

"To me too," Olivia said with a laugh. "But I love him, so I'll do it."

Faith had been working with Olivia for a few weeks now, and they'd developed a great friendship. She felt like she'd known her all her life, or like maybe this was what having a sister would feel like.

"So, we're going to sell these cookies at the carnival this weekend."

The HOPE carnival was both a fundraising event and a fun time for the kids they served. It would be down on the boardwalk on Saturday, and Faith had volunteered to be the face painter even though she had no perceivable artistic talents.

"Will Amelia be there?" Faith asked nonchalantly. Olivia smiled.

"Yes, of course."

"Have you heard anything about her situation lately?"

"Only that her mother got arrested again last weekend. Drug possession."

"Oh no. Where's Amelia?" Faith asked, her heart starting to race a bit.

"She's in a temporary foster situation. But I think they're hoping to find her a permanent situation soon. She's been tossed around a lot."

Faith sighed and closed her eyes. She wanted the best for Amelia. She had started spending a lot more time with her, eating lunch and occasionally taking her for ice cream.

"You really love that kid, don't you?"

Faith smiled sadly. "Shockingly, I do."

"Why is that a shock?"

"I guess I never thought of myself as the motherly type. I lost my mother when I was young, so I never really considered having my own kids as a life goal. And I was never a big fan of kids anyway."

"Sometimes life throws us the odd curveball."

"If Amelia gets adopted, will they be local?"

Olivia bit her lip. "Probably not. It could be anywhere in the state, or even out of state."

Faith looked back down at the paperwork she was working on and tried not to let Olivia see her tear-filled eyes. "Well, I hope they find her a great home then."

FAITH STEPPED INTO THE BOAT, the uneasy feeling of the water bobbing beneath her feet. Brandon had promised her that his friend was an experienced boater, but even now she was second guessing her decision to go on this little aquatic adventure.

"What if there aren't any dolphins?" she asked, turning back toward Brandon before stepping fully into the boat.

"So you think that dolphins may have disappeared from the ocean overnight?" he asked with a smile. "Then we should call the local news!"

"Very funny," she mumbled, finally making her way onto the small boat. "When you said dolphin cruise, I thought you meant in a larger boat."

Brandon put his hand on her back and ushered her into a padded seat before taking his spot next to her. "This is the best way to see them."

Faith peered over the side of the vessel. "But we're so close to the water."

"Zach has been taking people on these private tours for three years now, Faith. And, to be fair, he's only lost that one woman. But she really shouldn't have been hanging her hands over the side. I mean, who could've seen that shark coming?"

Faith's eyes grew wide and she started to stand up. Brandon broke out in hysterics and pulled her arm until she was sitting again.

"That wasn't funny!" she said, slapping his arm.

Still, she was going to keep her hands inside the boat at all times, just in case.

"Ya'll ready?" Zach, a beach bum if she ever saw one, asked.

"Absolutely!" Brandon answered, his enthusiasm not yet infectious. "This is going to be fun. I promise."

And she believed him, even though her heart was pounding as the small boat shot out toward the open water.

Within a few minutes, they slowed down and Zach started looking around with binoculars. When he spotted a small pod of dolphins, he started the boat up again slowly. To Faith's amazement, the dolphins began to follow them, jumping into the air in the wake behind them. She'd never seen anything so amazing.

"Look! There's one! And there's another one!" she said, giddily. She felt like a kid again she couldn't help but grin watching the creatures chase the boat with glee.

Brandon laughed as he watched her. "Pretty cool, huh?" he said over the load motor. She nodded and pulled out her phone to take video.

Faith couldn't remember a time when she felt so alive and free. Watching those dolphins jump into the air made her think about how tied down she'd felt her whole life. Trying to keep up appearances. Making sure to have the latest handbag and the most expensive shoes. How had she somehow missed out on the true joys in life?

She glanced over at Brandon who was smiling and talking to his friend, Zach, and for some reason thought about her father. Not her invisible biological father, but the one who'd raised her. The one who was currently sitting in a prison cell, probably not able to see daylight very much.

She thought about joy. Would he ever feel joy again? Did he deserve to? Her heart still ached for him, no matter how mad she was at how he'd wrecked both their lives and then abandoned her.

But suddenly, her life didn't feel wrecked anymore. Was it possible that she'd been holding onto the past so hard that she hadn't seen what was right in front of her? This new life. New friends. New work. And even Amelia. These amazing blessings that were falling into her lap left and right.

For weeks, she'd grieved over this fictional life she'd left behind in Virginia when in reality, she'd built a new, happier life in January Cove already.

"Thanks," she said to Brandon when he turned back around.

He smiled that dimpled smile of his, the one that probably gave female heart patients a few extra skipped beats. "Seeing you so happy is thanks enough."

She turned her attention back to the water. The

dolphins were falling further behind, and she waved at them as if they could see her.

"Where are we going now?"

"I thought Zach could take us by the island I told you about. Is that okay with you?"

"Sure," she said, ready for a little adventure. She didn't want this day to end. It was the first time in a long time she felt happy and relaxed.

A few minutes later, Zach pulled as far up to the island as he could. Brandon took off his shoes and jumped out into the knee deep water. He reached out with both hands to help Faith over the side as she tossed her sandals back into the boat.

"Zach is going to do a little fishing and come back to get us in a bit," Brandon explained as he helped her over the side. She slid down into the water, which was still pretty cool since springtime hadn't officially arrived yet.

They walked the short distance to the sand and sat down, each of them out of breath from fighting against the waves. As Zach drove off into the distance, Faith had a bit of anxiety well up inside of her. Here she was on a desolate island in the middle of nowhere with Brandon. She trusted him, but she'd trusted a few men in her past and that hadn't worked out so well.

"This is one of my favorite places in the world," Brandon said as he looked out at the water.

"It's beautiful."

"We had bonfires here a lot when I was a kid. After football games, we'd hitch a ride on the ferry and camp out."

"That sounds amazing. I wish I had grown up here."

"Yeah, there's something about January Cove that gets in your veins, and you never want to leave."

"But you did leave for awhile, right?" Faith asked.

"Touché," Brandon said with a chuckle. "That was something I felt called to do, though."

"Do you ever feel called back to the Middle East?"

Brandon looked at her. "I do. Sometimes the things I feel called to do conflict with each other."

She wasn't sure what that meant. "So what do you do when they conflict?"

"Well, that's when your heart and your gut have to have a meeting to decide what to do."

Faith laid back onto the warm sand and stared up at the blue sky. There were no clouds anywhere today, and the warmth of the sun was tempting her to take the best nap of her life.

Brandon laid back and joined her, staring up into the vastness of the heavens. They didn't speak for awhile. The only sounds were the waves and the squawking seagulls that would occasionally dive bomb down and snatch an unsuspecting fish from the ocean below.

Faith thought about how it must be to be that

fish. Swimming along. Thinking life is grand and then bam! Flying straight up into the air without knowing where you're going.

It was kind of morbid, but symbolic for what her life had been lately. Only the fish didn't get a new life in a great place. But the bird did get a fresh meal, she supposed. The circle of life.

"So, have you heard anything from your father yet?" Brandon suddenly asked, breaking her out of her enjoyable cocoon of happiness and tossing her butt right back into the real world that was all her own.

"No, I haven't. What made you think of that?" she asked, turning her head slightly toward him, trying to avoid the sunlight that was slipping under her fancy sunglasses.

"I've been wanting to ask you. Just didn't know how. I didn't want to upset you."

She appreciated the sentiment. "It doesn't upset me as much as it did when I first got here. I guess out of sight, out of mind." Even as she said it, she knew that it wasn't true. She thought about her father every single day. She worried about him. Was he safe? Was he well?

"I don't believe that for a minute, Faith. You love him, and I know you must be worried."

How did he read her mind like that? "Worrying doesn't do me any good, though. He's made it clear that he no longer wants me as his daughter." She turned her head back toward the sky and noticed a stray white, puffy cloud floating by. It was shaped like a poodle, she thought. Every time she saw a cloud, she wondered if her father was somewhere, peering out his tiny prison windows, looking at the same white blob in the sky. Probably not possible in scientific terms, she decided.

"Maybe you should try again. I'm sure he misses you."

"Look, Brandon, I love your optimism, but I can't go there again. I just have to let it go and hope that one day he reaches out to me. Until then, I have to move forward."

"I get it," he said before sitting up. "Looks like our ride is here." He pointed to Zach who was heading back to pick them up.

"That was quick," she said, wishing the afternoon wasn't over.

"Maybe we can do this again soon?" Brandon asked, a hopeful tone in his voice.

Faith smiled. "I'd like that."

∼

BRANDON LOOKED AT HIS WATCH. He was determined to get off work on time today. After all, he'd promised to help out at the carnival, and he wasn't about to let Olivia or the kids down. Or maybe he didn't want to let Faith down.

Since spending time with her on the boat and at the island, he realized that he was starting to have some serious feelings for her. But things were too up in the air. For one thing, he had no idea if she was going to stay in January Cove for good. He didn't know if she had any real feelings for him, other than a budding friendship. Plus, he'd recently been contacted about coming back to the Middle East to volunteer for at least another year. He hadn't told Faith that since he wasn't sure about his final decision.

A part of him felt like he had unfinished business in the region. He wanted to be able to help those people more, to save them from an uncertain fate. But, as his own mother had told him a million times, he couldn't save the world and sometimes he just needed to save himself.

Still, he felt conflicted. Should he take the opportunity to go back and help as many people as he could? Or should he stay in January Cove in the hopes that he could start a new life with Faith McLemore?

CHAPTER 8

aith stood under the small tent that she and Olivia had set up for face painting. It was just big enough for two chairs and a small table filled with a bright assortment of paints. The sun was really beating down today, spring now in full force in January Cove.

She could smell the salty sea air as it blew gently across the pier, and it felt like home. She loved this place and these new people. It was amazing that she was starting to feel like January Cove was where she was always meant to be. It had been like coming home.

Of course, it was probably her original home. Somewhere among the moss covered trees and sandy beaches, her biological mother had probably walked. She looked around at the large crowd of people enjoying the carnival and wondered if her birth mother was somewhere out there.

She had come to January Cove to find her birth mother in the first place, yet she'd put that on the back burner lately. Being busy with volunteer work and spending time with Brandon kept her mind occupied, but it had also kept her from finding out the truth.

Faith wanted to know more about her mother, but the truth was that she was scared. What if she was dead? What if she wasn't a good person? And worst of all, what if she just didn't want to meet her? What if she was just another person who wanted to abandon her?

"I want a butterfly, please!" the perky little girl demanded as she plopped down in the chair in front of Faith.

"I'm sorry, what?"

"Right here, on this cheek," the little girl said, pointing at her pudgy left cheek. Her mother stood next to her, slight confusion on her face.

"Oh. Right," Faith said, trying to refocus her mind on the task at hand. "Blue or pink?"

"Pink, of course," the little girl said, rolling her eyes. Faith began painting, trying not to let her mind wander again. When she finished, the little girl squealed with delight as she looked into the hand mirror and then ran off into the crowd, her mother calling after her.

"You're doing a great job, Faith," Olivia said as she came around the corner.

"Thank you, but I don't think I'll be applying for art school anytime soon," she said with a laugh. "How's it going for you over there?"

"We're selling cakes and cupcakes left and right. Sweet Cakes bakery really helped us out today."

"That's great. Hopefully we're raising a lot of money."

"We definitely are," Olivia said with a smile. "Oh, it looks like you have a customer," she said before walking away.

Faith turned to see Brandon sitting in the chair in front of her. Their faces were inches apart, and the feeling of electricity between them jolted her for a moment.

"Oh, hi. You scared me," she said shakily as she moved back a few inches. Brandon smiled.

"I'd like a dragon, please."

"What?"

"Right... here," he said, pointing to his right cheek and leaning forward.

"Brandon, I'm not painting a dragon on your cheek. This booth is for the children!" she chided.

He stood up and looked at the tent, carefully walking around it and then sitting back down. "Nope. Nothing says this is just for kids."

She stared at him in disbelief. Here was this

skilled physician, still in his scrubs from work, demanding a dragon be painted on his face.

"Fine. But I'll warn you that I'm not an artist, and I have no idea how to paint a dragon."

He leaned in closer again. "I'll take my chances."

She dabbed some paint onto her brush and cleared her throat before leaning toward him. How in the world was she supposed to paint his face with her hand shaking so bad?

"Okay, stay still," she said softly as she touched the brush to his skin. She quickly realized that she'd have to use her other hand to hold his face in place, so she slid her fingers up under his jaw.

Oh dear Lord. His skin was so warm, and she could smell his cologne. Chills ran down from her hand all the way to her heart, and she was afraid he'd notice the redness appearing on her cheeks soon. Who knew stubble could feel so sexy in your hand?

"Everything okay?" he asked.

"Yes, why?" she responded, her voice two octaves higher. She was desperately trying not to make eye contact and instead focus on the work at hand.

"You seem a little shaky."

If she didn't know better, she'd have thought he was enjoying her discomfort. There was a slight smile on his face, and although it was extremely attractive, it led her to believe he was messing with her a bit. But for what purpose?

As she ran her fingers across his skin, she had to wonder what it would feel to touch his face all the time? Why wasn't some woman scooping this man up? If she leaned in and kissed his jawline, would he notice?

She wasn't ready for this. She wasn't ready for actual feelings. Her life was a mess. What did she even bring to the table for a guy like him? She had no job. No home. No idea who her family was.

Nope, she wasn't going there. She wasn't going to even consider the fact that her hand was trembling because she had a strong desire to grab his face and plant a big wet kiss on those smiling lips of his. She cared way too much about Brandon as a person to mess up his life with her broken heart.

Faith looked at her work so far. It was messy and smeared. Ugh. She needed to start over. She grabbed a wet cloth and brushed it across his face.

"What're you doing?" he asked.

"I messed up."

He chuckled and turned to face her. "It's all in good fun, Faith. Don't stress out about it."

His voice was soft and calming to her. "It looked like a blob that threw up another blob."

Brandon laughed. "Way to sell it."

Faith had to smile at that. He had a way of making her feel better. "Let me try again."

This time she was determined to stay focused. No more thoughts of kissing or touching or long walks on the beach with their three children in tow....

A few minutes later, she was finished. And she was pretty proud of her creation. She grabbed the mirror and handed it to him, a smile spreading across her face.

"Pretty good, huh?"

Brandon looked, his eyes wide, and then laughed out loud. Faith was confused.

"What's wrong?" she asked.

"Um, Faith, this is Barney."

"What?"

"The cartoon character. The big purple dinosaur."

She sat for a moment, trying to take in his words. Dinosaur. Oh crap. Dinosaurs were most definitely not dragons.

"Oh my gosh... You said dragon. And I painted a big purple dinosaur on your cheek." Now *her* cheeks were turning red.

Brandon continued cackling with laughter until tears were running down his cheeks. She felt like an idiot. When he finally caught his breath, he put his hands on her shoulders.

"Faith McLemore, you make life so much fun."

Her breath caught in her throat. No one had ever said anything like that to her. All of the other men in her life had said she made life more expensive, maybe, but not more fun.

"Sorry about the dinosaur. Let me help you get that off," she said as Brandon stood up.

Brandon covered his cheek. "No way! I love it!"

"No, you don't. No man wants to walk around with that on his cheek. Here, you can use this."

Brandon took the cloth from her hand and put it on the table. "Faith, I may never wash this cheek again now that you've painted this work of art on it."

"Very funny."

"Is that the purple dinosaur?" Amelia asked from the other side of the tent.

"Oh, hey, Amelia! Yes, it is a Faith McLemore original. Would you like one?" Brandon asked, smiling as he cut his eyes back in Faith's direction.

"No thanks. But can you do roller skates?"

"Roller skates? Do you like skating?" Faith asked.

Amelia walked over slowly and sat in the chair. "Yeah. I love skating."

"Cool. Maybe we can go sometime," Faith said hopefully.

"Maybe. But I might be leaving soon."

Faith's heart skipped a beat. "Really? Why is that?" She sat down in her chair and waited for Amelia to answer.

"My case worker said no one here really wants me so I might have to go somewhere in another state."

Faith was angry. No one wants her? Who says that to a child? She wanted to get up and hunt this person down, and she'd do a lot more than paint a dinosaur on their face!

"Amelia, I'm so sorry someone said that to you. I'm sure so many people would want you as their daughter."

Amelia looked up at Faith. "I don't think anyone wants me."

Faith looked up at Brandon, who was still standing at the edge of the tent. Gone was his smile, and it was replaced by a look of shock. Faith felt nauseous.

"Well, today is a day for fun, right?" Brandon suddenly said.

"I guess so," Amelia responded.

"And since you're here with HOPE today, Faith and I are going to make sure you have the most fun today that you've ever had!"

Faith looked back up at him, unsure of what he was planning. But if she knew anything about Brandon, it was that he always had a plan.

"Ya'll get to work on that amazing cheek artwork, and I'll be back in a flash, okay?" Before Faith could respond, Brandon was trotting off into the crowd.

"Is he your husband?" Amelia asked as Faith started painting.

"No, he's not," Faith said with a giggle.

"Your boyfriend?"

"Nope. Just a friend."

"Yeah right," Amelia said, rolling her eyes.

"Excuse me?"

"You like him."

"I do like him. That's why he's my friend." Why were kids so dang perceptive?

"I think you like him as more than a friend, Miss Faith."

"Oh yeah? And why do you think that?" Faith asked as she started working on the wheels of the skates.

"Because you look at him like one of those puppies down at the shelter."

Faith laughed. "And how is that?"

"Like you want him to pick you up and carry you away," Amelia said giggling.

"Well, I don't feel like a shelter puppy. Dr. James is just my friend."

"If you say so."

"I say so."

Faith continued painting as Amelia talked. She told her about how HOPE was helping her with tutoring for math and how her teacher said she was smart. Faith listened, taking in every word in fear that Amelia would just be gone one day soon.

"So, what's your favorite color?" Faith asked as she worked. It had taken her a few weeks to get Amelia to open up at all, so having a conversation with her felt like a victory.

"Pink."

Faith worked to put as much pink as possible

into her design. She was getting the hang of this face painting thing. Too bad she couldn't make a career of it.

"What's your favorite color?" Amelia asked.

"Sky blue. Just like the color above us right now."

Amelia cut her eyes to the sky. "I like it when there aren't any clouds."

"Me too," Faith said as she put the finishing touches on the skates she was painting.

"I'm going to miss it here."

Faith put down her brush and took in a deep breath. "Sweetie, you don't know if you're even leaving yet."

"Yeah, I do. Nobody wants me here. Maybe it's better that I leave anyway."

"That's not true, Amelia," Faith said, turning her around in the chair. "I want you."

"You do?" The hopefulness in her voice was heartbreaking. Faith wished she could take back her words.

"I do, Amelia, but I can't adopt you."

Amelia's face fell. "Oh." She turned back around in her seat, slouched down more with her arms crossed around her body. It wasn't the body language of someone who was angry, but of someone who was protecting herself.

"You don't understand, but they wouldn't let me adopt you even if I wanted to. You see, I'm new in town and I don't have a job or a place to live. I stay at the inn." Faith stammered out the words, trying like crazy to make the little girl understand.

"Everything okay here?" Olivia asked as she walked into the tent and felt the tension in the air.

Faith looked up at her. "Um, yeah. Everything is fine."

Olivia looked concerned but didn't push further. "So, Brandon tells me you need a break. Addy is coming over to take your paintbrushes."

"What?"

"Hey, ladies. Ready to go?" Brandon asked as he walked over. He'd changed his clothes to a more suitable pair of shorts and a polo shirt.

"Go where?" Faith was utterly confused.

"I told you. We're having a day of fun!"

She didn't feel like having fun right now. She felt like crying and running off with Amelia under her arm.

"But Olivia needs me here, Brandon."

"No, she doesn't. I'm a trained face painter," Addy said with a smile as she arrived beside the tent. "Go on. Have a fun day!"

Faith looked at Amelia. The little girl deserved a fun day that was all about her. Odds were no one had ever done something like this for her before, and leave it to Brandon to plan this.

"Okay. Thanks, Addy. I really appreciate it."

Addy hugged Faith. "He's a great guy. Enjoy your date," she whispered in Faith's ear.

"It's not a date," Faith whispered back. Addy just smiled and waved as they walked away with Amelia between them.

~

BRANDON WAS STUFFED. Between the hot dogs and ice cream he'd had in the last couple of hours, he felt like he needed a nice long nap. But he wasn't going to let either one of these women down.

Amelia was a great kid. Full of spunk and joy, he had a hard time understanding how anyone wouldn't want her as their daughter. He'd always dreamed of having a daughter, or actually two daughters and one son. For as long as Brandon could remember, this was his dream family. Just the five of them conquering the world.

But he was nowhere close to living that dream. He was painfully single. Nights were the hardest for him. He was lonely in his nice little beach house, and he'd lie in bed thinking about the future and wondering if he'd ever be a husband and father. Most guys his age were either already married with kids or at least engaged. And though his married friends often told him to enjoy bachelorhood more, he wasn't interested in hanging out in bars or perusing the online dating world.

He wanted his own family. It was another thing to consider when he thought about going back overseas. He wanted to help people. He wanted to make a difference in their lives. But he also, maybe selfishly in his eyes, wanted a certain kind of life for himself. It was a tough balancing act.

"She's having a great time, isn't she?" Faith asked again. She was so worried Amelia wasn't having fun even though the kid had been smiling since the first carousel ride.

"Yes, she's having a blast," Brandon whispered back. He loved whispering in her ear. Her hair was blowing in the ocean breeze, and he could smell what appeared to be strawberry scented shampoo.

"All thanks to you," she said, looking up at him. She really was a beautiful woman. Smart. Caring. *Stop it, Brandon. Don't do this to yourself.*

"And you," he said. She smiled. And when she smiled, he melted a little inside. This was bad.

"Look at her. She's got quite an arm," Faith said, pointing at Amelia who was currently flinging baseballs at targets, trying to win a giant stuffed pink bear she'd been eyeing all day.

"If she doesn't get it, I will," Brandon said, flexing his muscles. "Played baseball all four years in…"

"Got it!" Amelia yelled out, jumping up and down with a huge grin on her face.

Faith turned around and laughed at Brandon. "Guess you'll have to use those guns for something else."

His first thought was picking her up and carrying

her down the beach. *Stop it, Brandon!* Yeah, that wasn't working.

~

FAITH WALKED DOWN THE BEACH, the edges of the water touching her toes over and over before retreating. It was quiet, all except the faint sounds of people still milling about on the pier behind them, taking in the final moments of the yearly carnival.

Olivia had taken Amelia back to the group home she was currently in while waiting for placement. As Faith had watched her walk away, not knowing when or if she'd see her again, her heart had felt as if it literally might break into pieces. Thankfully, Brandon had pulled her away and invited her for a walk on the beach.

But even the beauty of the ocean and the pink sky peeking up over the horizon wasn't doing anything to improve her mood. She felt utterly helpless.

"I know you're worried, Faith," Brandon finally said.

She sighed. "I am. But worrying won't do me any good. I just hope they find Amelia a good, stable home with parents who love her."

"Me too," he said, adding his own sigh. He stopped and touched her arm. She turned to face him, and he put his hands on her shoulders. "You've done good things for her, Faith. And for the other HOPE kids. I'm proud of you."

She had no idea why those words made her tear up, but they did. The fact that someone, especially Brandon, was actually proud of her meant everything. He'd been a virtual stranger a few weeks ago, but now he was the best friend she'd ever had.

"Thank you," she said softly. And then everything started moving in slow motion as she saw him leaning in, his eyes staring at hers. Did she want him to kiss her? Was this a good idea? And how was she having all of these lucid thoughts in the split second before his lips would be touching hers...

"Excuse me, can you take a picture of us?" An unfamiliar voice broke the moment open like a stick of dynamite before Brandon's lips could make it to their destination. "Sorry to interrupt, but we're trying to get a family picture in front of the sunset," the woman said, pointing to her husband and two small children behind her. She held out her phone to Faith, who was frozen in place, so Brandon reached around and took it.

"Sure. I'd be glad to," Brandon said, smiling at the woman. He quickly snapped a picture, and watched as they moved on down the beach.

Faith stood there, unsure of what to say. "Cute kids," she finally stammered.

"Yeah. Kids are cute." Brandon paused for a

moment and then burst out laughing. "And the parents sure can ruin a mood, huh?"

Faith giggled. "Just a bit."

"Maybe it's for the best. I mean, you looked a little terrified."

"I did?" She said as they started walking again.

"You looked like a deer in the headlights, as they say."

"Well, you seemed a little hesitant yourself," she said, not really meaning it but wanting to see his reaction.

"Doubtful."

"Oh really? You weren't hesitant about kissing me?"

There. She'd said it. She'd blurted out the great big kissing elephant in the room. Brandon stopped and turned to her, his arms crossed against his chest.

"I wasn't the least bit hesitant about kissing you, Faith."

She couldn't breathe for a moment as he just looked at her. "I don't think I'm ready for this." She heard the words fall out of her mouth and instantly regretted them. She was ready. She did want to plant a big wet kiss on Brandon's lips, so why was she saying this?

Brandon's face fell a bit, but he quickly recovered with his amazing, approachable smile. "You've been through a lot lately. I can understand that. Can't blame a guy for trying, right?"

She let out a nervous laugh, and they started walking again. "I guess not."

They made their way down the beach and between a couple of houses until they were on the main street leading to Addy's Inn. Faith felt more uncomfortable than she'd felt in her life, and she just wanted to scurry upstairs and curl into the fetal position until morning.

"Listen, about that awkward moment on the beach..." Brandon said.

Faith glanced up at the inn. So close, yet so far. "Let's just forget it."

"I just want to say something."

"Okay."

Brandon put his hands on her shoulders again. This was a recipe for disaster as she wanted to scoot forward and lay her head on his chest just to see how it felt.

"We're friends, Faith, and I wouldn't ever do anything to screw that up. But let me just say that the invitation is always open. Got it?"

Her face started to flush. "Got it," she eked out before turning to head inside. She opened the door and peeked out the stained glass window insert to watch Brandon walk down the road.

CHAPTER 9

F aith walked down the sidewalk, looking in each of the store windows. She'd been in January Cove for months now, but she'd never taken the time to visit all of the local shops. One in particular she'd been avoiding just because she knew she'd put on an extra ten pounds if she got addicted, and that was Sweet Cakes.

Everyone in town had been talking about the amazing desserts at Laura Bennett's bakery, so she decided today was the day. After all, it was her birthday, and she didn't have any special plans.

She'd been thinking more and more about her birthmother today. Being that this was her first birthday knowing she was adopted, a part of her felt like it was missing. She wanted to find her birthmother, or any family member really, but that had been pushed to the back of her mind lately as she focused on working at HOPE.

Still, if she planned to stay in January Cove, she had to get a real, paying job soon. And that would mean less volunteer time, which made her sad.

Faith pulled the door open to Sweet Cakes and was surprised to see Olivia sitting at a table in the corner alone. Her always vibrant friend was solemn, her face almost blank, as she sat there with a cupcake in front of her.

"Olivia? You okay?"

Olivia looked up, surprised to see Faith standing there. "Oh. Hey, Faith. Yeah, I'm fine."

Faith pulled out the chair across from her and sat down. "You don't look fine. Did something happen?"

"Just having a tough day. But it'll pass, and I'll be okay."

"Wanna talk about it?" Faith prodded.

Olivia smiled sadly. "No. But thank you. It's just something I have to deal with."

Faith hoped it wasn't related to her marriage. Or what if it was about one of the kids?

"Is it about Amelia?" Faith finally asked, unable to hold in her concern.

Olivia smiled and touched her hand. "No, honey. She's still in the group home. The judge is making final decisions on the case next week."

"Oh."

"I know you're invested in Amelia. To be honest,

I'm a bit worried about how you'll react if and when she gets adopted."

"I have to be okay with it," Faith said. "I mean, I want what's best for her."

"So what are you doing here today?" Olivia asked, putting on a fake smile.

"Don't tell anyone, but it's my birthday," Faith said.

"Oh, happy birthday!" Olivia said, squeezing Faith's hand. "And here's your cake!" She slid the chocolate cupcake across the table toward Faith.

"I'm not eating your cupcake!"

"Oh, I never eat it anyway."

"I don't understand. You come here, order a cupcake, look at it and then don't eat it?"

Olivia laughed. "Long story, don't ask."

"Okay..."

"But I do have a birthday present for you!"

"You didn't know it was my birthday, Liv."

"I know, but this is perfect timing. I was going to come by Addy's today to ask you something."

"What?"

"Would you be interested in a full time position at HOPE?"

Faith's heart skipped a beat. Working at HOPE would be a dream for her. "Really? But how can you afford that?"

"Well, Susan is leaving. Her husband got transferred to Texas, and that leaves the

Assistant Director position open. You'd be perfect, Faith."

"Assistant Director? Really?" Faith couldn't get the smile off her face. This meant everything! She could keep working with Olivia and the kids, but get paid for it. This was her dream job.

Wait. Her dream job? She'd never had a dream job until she'd arrived in January Cove. Her life had changed so much in recent months that it was barely recognizable to her.

"I accept!" she said, still beaming. "Thank you so much, Olivia. You have no idea what this means to me."

"Well, I hope you don't mind that I told Brandon that I was going to offer the job to you. He'd like to have a celebratory dinner party tomorrow night. Is that okay?"

"Of course! I'm just ecstatic. I have to go tell Addy."

"Not before you eat your birthday cake," Olivia said, pushing the cupcake closer to her.

"Fine. But not unless you join me," Faith said, squinting her eyes at Olivia.

"Okay, but this is really breaking my tradition," she said as she pinched off one side of the dessert.

~

BRANDON HAD THROWN the perfect dinner party to celebrate Faith's new job. Many of the Parker family were there, and of course Olivia was there.

"Dinner was fab, as always," Olivia said to Brandon as she headed for the front door.

"Thanks for helping me organize it," he said, giving her a quick hug.

"See you at work on Monday," Olivia said to Faith.

"I'll be there bright and early, boss," she said, giving her best military salute.

They watched Olivia walk to her car and drive away. The house was now empty, and that always presented a challenge to Faith. The "almost kiss" on the beach had made things a little awkward for a few days, but before she knew it, they were right back to where they were.

"Let me help clean up," Faith said.

Brandon waved his hand. "No, this was your party. You don't clean up at your own party."

"I don't mind, really."

He blocked the doorway to the kitchen. "Nope. You go plop down in front of the TV, and let me finish up. I'll put on a pot of coffee if you'll stay awhile?"

"Sure. Sounds good."

"Go sit. One of those singing TV shows is on. I know you like those."

Faith smiled. "You know me so well."

"I try."

She walked to the other side of the house and sat down in one of the big fluffy armchairs. As she watched Brandon from across the open floorplan, she tried to imagine what it might be like if they were married. He'd do the dishes, she'd sit around trying to look pretty. Sounded like a fair compromise.

"I'm going to take this trash out," Brandon called from the kitchen. Faith nodded.

"Where is the remote? This thing is so loud," she said to herself. She stood and walked around the room. She picked up a magazine thinking maybe it was underneath, but instead she found a pad of paper. On it there were details about travel to the Middle East and the name of the charity Brandon had worked with in the region.

"Huh. This must be a very old pad of paper," she said to herself again. Her attention was diverted by a loud ding, and she realized it was Brandon's cell phone. An unknown person had texted him. She knew she shouldn't have looked, but she couldn't help herself so she glanced at it.

I know you don't want to tell Faith about the plans you've made for your future, but time is ticking and she's going to find out soon. Maybe you should...

"I'm back," Brandon called as he came back into the house. He stopped and looked at Faith. "Everything okay?"

She swallowed and opened her eyes wide. "Yeah, of course. Listen, I need to leave."

"What? Why? I just put on the coffee."

"I know, and I'm so sorry but I'm just so tired. And I've got work coming up so I need to be fresh, ya know?" She started walking around the living room, searching for her purse while fake yawning.

"Faith, is something wrong? You're acting a little... frantic."

"I'm fine. Really."

"Then stay. Please. Just for coffee?"

She didn't want to start a whole "thing". He wasn't her boyfriend anyway, so what say so did she have in his life? In her mind, he tried to kiss her, she rebuffed him and now he was planning to leave town. Why did she always drive the men in her life away?

"Okay. But then I really need to get home. It's getting late."

"It's eight-thirty on a Saturday night, Faith."

She looked at her watch. "Yep."

He furrowed his eyebrows, still obviously unsure of what was going on with her. "Alrighty then. I'm going to get the coffee ready. You just chill out in there, and I'll be in shortly."

Faith went back to the room, but this time sat on the end of the love seat next to the table. She felt no pride as she craned her head to see if more texts had come in.

Keeping this a secret is only going to cause you more stress. I think you just need to tell her because this is a pretty big change you're making. Maybe she won't be okay with it...

Oh, God. He was definitely leaving January Cove and going back to the Middle East. There was no other way to interpret the messages. And who were they from? And why did the person even know her name? Her heart sank as she thought about life in January Cove without Brandon.

"Coffee with soy milk and extra sugar," Brandon said, handing her the cup and saucer. "Oh, there's my phone. I've been looking for it all night."

"Phone? Oh. I didn't even see it," she said, worried that he'd look at her face and realize she was a terrible poker player.

Brandon sat down across from her in one of the chairs. "So, are you excited about your new job?"

She was thankful he seemed to be unaware of what she'd just seen and read. "Yes. Definitely."

"I know you'll do great, Faith. You're a perfect fit at HOPE."

"Thanks."

"So, listen... Olivia told me I missed your birthday yesterday? Why didn't you say anything?"

"It was just a birthday. No big deal."

"Well, I do actually have a gift for you. I hope you like it," he said, pulling a white envelope out if his pocket and handing it to her.

"What's this?"

"Open it." Brandon was all smiles as he waited for her to read the contents.

Faith slowly opened the envelope which revealed a letter inside. She immediately recognized the handwriting. Her father.

"My Dad?"

"Yep," Brandon said, his smile growing wider.

"But I don't understand. How did you get a letter from my Dad?"

"Well, I know how it's been bothering you that he wouldn't allow contact. So I reached out to a buddy of mine up that way. He knows a guard at the prison, so I wrote him a letter and they…"

"Are you kidding me right now?" she said, her face turning red from anger.

"What? Faith, I don't understand… You're mad at me?"

"Of course I'm mad! You went behind my back and contacted my louse of a father without asking me first?"

"But you would've said no."

"And that wasn't a clue that you shouldn't do that? I told you on the island that I wanted to leave it alone until he reached out to me, if he ever did."

"I was only trying to help you, Faith."

"I don't need your help or anyone else's! I'm a grown woman. What you did was a betrayal of my trust, Brandon." She stood up, grabbed her purse and moved swiftly to the front door.

"Faith, I'm sorry. I thought I was doing a good thing…" Brandon said behind her.

"Thanks for dinner, Brandon. But please, for the love of God, stay out of my personal life, okay?" She slammed the door behind her and walked down the road toward Addy's.

～

"I HONESTLY DON'T KNOW what I did wrong, Liv," Brandon said as he sat with Olivia on his back deck. The waves were particularly hostile today, which went perfectly with his last interaction with Faith. He'd never seen her that angry before.

"I guess it invaded her privacy. She seems to be hurt by things in her past, so maybe it's got something to do with that."

Brandon hesitated for a moment. "She hasn't told you why she's in January Cove, has she?"

"No. I thought she just moved here for a new start or something. She did tell me about her father being in prison, but that was only recently."

"I probably shouldn't tell you this, but Faith is here to find her birthmother. When her father went to jail, she found out she'd been adopted as a baby."

Olivia looked stunned. "Really? Why wouldn't she mention that?"

"She just got so invested in HOPE and Amelia that I think she's procrastinating on the search. It was a dead end. That's why I contacted her father. I thought maybe he knew more. I don't think he knows anything else, but I'd hoped they could mend fences a bit too."

"Your heart was in the right place. So, her birthmother was from right here in January Cove, huh?"

"Seems that way. She grew up in Virginia. Not sure how she got all the way up there from this tiny town, though."

Olivia was quiet for a moment. "And she couldn't find any information?"

"Nope. Just that her birthmother was really young at the time. No other real information."

"What's she going to do now?"

"Well, before she bit my head off, I helped her do one of those DNA test kits she ordered in the mail. They take awhile to come back with results, though."

"Faith's a great person. I'm sure she'll cool off soon and forgive you. After all, I think she has a little crush on the dashing Dr. Brandon James."

Brandon laughed. "Not even my medical degree could've saved me on this one."

"Give her time and a little space. She'll come around. Besides, you've got a lot of changes coming up in your own life, right?"

"Right. And I've never been more scared either."

FAITH SAT in her room at Addy's staring at the letter. She hadn't read it yet. Couldn't bring herself to think about what Jim McLemore had written. Did she want an apology? Did she want to know he was okay? She didn't know what she wanted anymore.

Tomorrow she'd start her new job at HOPE. She'd been excited about it just twenty-four hours before, but now she didn't know how to feel about anything in her life, especially Brandon.

She couldn't remember a time when she'd been more angry at someone, well maybe except for her father. Still, she felt a little guilty for lashing out at Brandon like she did. He'd done a stupid thing, in her opinion, but he'd done it for her out of the goodness of his heart.

He had no way of knowing that she was like a scalded dog having read his text messages. And she had been wrong to read them, so who was she to judge him?

It was all so confusing, but the one thing that was for certain was there was a letter sitting on her desk from the father who'd raised her and loved her. She needed to read it and see if he'd provided any more information on her birthmother.

She slowly walked across the room and picked it up, bringing it to her nose for a brief second in the hopes that it smelled like her father's cologne. Instead, it smelled stale and a little bit like hot dogs.

She opened it, running her fingers across his handwriting. It looked the same as always - small and boxy.

Dear Faith,

My God, how I've missed you. I'm so sorry I cut off communication with you, but I thought it was best at the time. I didn't want you to feel obligated to take care of me anymore, Faith. I thought I was making it easier for you, but your friend tells me I tore your heart out.

Please forgive me.

I've unblocked everything, and I hope you'll write me back some day. I hear you're living the beach life and doing great things in January Cove. I know your birth-mother would be proud that you're giving back in her town, and I sure am proud of you too.

Faith, I wish I knew more about your birthmother, but I don't. But I have no doubt that your friend cares a lot about you and will help you find the answers you seek.

I hope you'll write me back because I long to hear from you, even if it's just in letter form. I miss you so much, and I hope there's still a place for me in your life. If not, I'll understand. You need to do what's best for you. That's really all I want.

Well, I have to go. It's time to eat lunch, and it's hot dog day here. If you don't get first in line, you end up with shriveled up hot dogs which taste worse than they look.

I love you, my baby girl.

Dad

Faith hadn't realized how hard she was crying until she saw two tears fall onto the page and smudge the ink. He still loved her. She'd been so mad at him all these months that she'd forgotten how much she still loved him too.

CHAPTER 10

Faith sat at her new desk and looked out the window. She felt so official now even though her workload was much the same. At least now there would be a paycheck associated with her hard work.

Never in her life had she felt so needed as she did at HOPE. She felt like the kids needed her, but also Olivia as she seemed to be struggling with something lately.

"Lunch?" Olivia said as she handed Faith a bag from the local deli. "Don't worry. It's vegan."

Faith smiled. "You know me so well."

Olivia sat in the chair across from her desk and pulled out her salad. "So, how's your first day going so far?"

"Well, I spoke to a couple of the teachers at the school. Maggie and Jose are both improving in their grades since we started the new tutoring program. And I'm planning a special picnic at the park on Elm just after Easter."

"Wow! You've been busy."

"I need to keep busy right now, so that's a good thing." Faith took a bite of her sandwich and closed her eyes. "This is amazing."

"Brandon told me what he did."

Faith stopped chewing. "And did he tell you I freaked out?"

"Not in those words... but yes."

"It just made me mad that he went behind my back, Liv."

"I know it did, Faith, but you know Brandon is a great guy. And he only did it because he was trying to help."

"I know."

"So, was your father any help?"

Faith froze. "Any help for what?"

Olivia's eyes grew wide. "Oh jeez..."

"Oh my gosh! He told you? Can that man keep his mouth shut about anything?"

"Faith, he just wants to help you."

"I didn't want people to know."

"Why? We've become friends, right?"

"Of course," Faith said, feeling bad that Olivia was hurt she hadn't told her. "I just didn't want people to pity me."

"No one would pity you for being adopted, Faith."

"I guess you're right."

"So did your Dad have any other information?" Olivia asked again.

"No. Not a bit."

"I'm sorry. But Brandon said the DNA testing would be back soon. Maybe that will lead to something?"

"Maybe. I'm trying not to get my hopes up. Besides, I have plenty to keep me busy here."

"Are you going to forgive Brandon?"

Faith sat quietly for a moment. "It's more than this, Olivia. Can you keep a secret?"

"Sure."

"I think Brandon is moving back to the Middle East. I accidentally saw some messages on his cell phone."

"You looked at his text messages?"

Faith stilled for a moment. How stupid was it to tell her new boss that she spied on someone's text messages? Duh.

"Not on purpose. I was looking for the remote to his TV. Anyway, there were notes beside his phone about the Middle East charity he worked with, and then the texts…"

"But, Faith, it sounds like you don't know that for certain." Olivia seemed to know something, or maybe she was just trying to play mediator. Either way, Faith decided it was best not to interrogate her boss on her first day at a new job.

"Look, I know he's your friend. And he's my friend. And I'll forgive him. But that's it. I almost let myself get a little too invested in thinking about a future..." Faith purposely trailed off because she didn't want to admit to too much.

Thankfully, the ringing phone on her desk cut the conversation short.

~

BRANDON WALKED out of the hospital toward the physician's parking lot. It was a beautiful day with clear blue skies, and he wished he could spend it with Faith. She hadn't spoken to him in days, and he missed her.

"Brandon?" Olivia called out from across the parking lot. She caught up to him, winded from running across the hot pavement.

"Liv? You okay?"

"I'm fine, but I think you need to tell Faith about your plans."

"No way. She's already mad at me, and if this plan goes off track then..."

"I know, but she has totally the wrong idea."

"What idea does she have?"

Olivia took in a deep breath and then sighed. "I

can't say. I promised. But I'm afraid it's going to ruin any chance you have of a future with her."

"Well, that's not helpful at all if you can't tell me anything."

"Look, all I can say is that you need to talk to her. Try to get her to understand why you contacted her father. I think she'll forgive you for that. But she still has assumptions about other things."

"Your vagueness astounds me, Liv."

"I'm sorry. She's my friend, and I just can't break her confidence."

"I understand. Thanks for catching up with me. I think her DNA results will come in this week, so that will give me a reason to meet up with her."

Olivia stared at him for a moment. "This week. Really? Wow. Okay. Well, let me know what ya'll find out, okay?"

"Will do."

Brandon drove away and watched Olivia stand there for a moment before she walked slowly across the parking lot. The women in this town were suddenly acting really squirrelly.

～

FAITH TURNED off the lights in her office and grabbed her purse. She was looking forward to a night of Netflix and ice cream, followed by a hot bath and hopefully sweet dreams. As she pulled the door to the office closed behind her, she realized her plans might just get derailed.

"Brandon, what're you doing here?"

He was standing just outside of the office on the sidewalk. Faith had told Olivia to go home early since she had a headache and looked stressed. Now she was stressed too.

"We need to talk."

"Okay. About what?"

"Care to take a walk with me?"

"Brandon, I don't…"

"Come on. Just to the pier. We can sit on a bench and take in some of that ocean breeze you love so much."

She sucked in a deep breath and let it out before nodding. "Let me put my stuff in my car."

They walked quietly down the road, the sound of sea gulls and the occasional car the only things disrupting their trip. It was awkward. She really wanted that ice cream.

When they got to the pier, they both sat down and stared out at the ocean for a few moments. It was a beautiful day, as most days were in January Cove. No storms looming. No puffy white clouds. Just blue ocean touching blue sky.

"I'm sorry, Faith. I didn't mean to hurt you or make you angry by contacting your father," he said as he rubbed his hands together in his lap. "I thought I was helping, but it's obvious that I didn't. I hope you can forgive me. Sometimes I get a little overzealous trying to help people I care about."

"You care about me?" Faith said, trying not to make eye contact.

"More than you realize." Her heart was starting to pound. No no no! She couldn't get reeled in. He was leaving. She would never ask him to stay for her. People needed him across the world, and she'd never stand in his way.

"I forgive you, Brandon. I know you were trying to help. And honestly, it did help."

He turned slightly to face her. "Really? How?"

"Well, he didn't know anything about my birth-mother, unfortunately. But he said he missed me, and he wanted to hear from me. I'm planning to write him a letter soon... when I'm ready."

"Oh, Faith, that's great. I'm so happy for you," he said, touching her knee. Faith moved her leg slightly, just enough that his hand fell away. Brandon cleared his throat.

"Sorry."

"Look, Brandon, I appreciate everything you've done for me. And I want to be friends. But right now everything feels kind of weird between us. I don't know how to fix that. I don't even know if it can be fixed," she said, still trying not to look at him. Because if she looked at him, she might want to kiss him. And then her heart would be broken when he left. Oh, who was she kidding? Her heart was going to be broken no matter what. The story of her life.

"I know I did something wrong, Faith, but you seem upset about something else. Please, just tell me what it is."

Her gut churned. Should she be honest and tell him about reading the texts? Or should she just let him go on thinking it was the letter to her father that broke up their promising relationship?

"I know you're leaving."

Brandon cocked his head. "What?"

"I accidentally saw the notepad at your house about the Middle East charity. And then your phone dinged, and I saw some texts."

"You read my texts?" He sounded irritated, but not angry.

"Not on purpose. Well, the first time it wasn't on purpose. The second time was definitely on purpose."

"Faith, I don't think you understand…"

She put her hand up. "I do understand, Brandon. I know that place and those people mean everything to you, and I would never stand in the way…"

"But, it's not what you…"

"Just tell me the date."

"What date?"

"The date you're leaving."

Brandon sat for a moment and looked like he was pondering something. "Two weeks. It's tentative, but yes my life is going to change big time in about two weeks."

Faith sucked in a breath through her nose and blew it slowly out of her mouth. It was the one yoga trick that she still used. Downward dog always gave her a headache.

"I want you to know that I appreciate your friendship. It really helped me make January Cove my home. And I want the best for you. I know you'll make a huge difference in a lot of lives." She was trying to be the bigger person, but she really wanted to fall to the ground, grab his leg and beg him not to go. Not her finest moment.

"Faith, I really think I need to explain…"

"Please don't. Why did you want to see me? Was it just to apologize?"

He pulled an envelope out of his shirt pocket and unfolded it.

"Oh no. The last time you handed me an envelope, it didn't work out so well," she said.

Brandon laughed. "This one you already knew about. It's the DNA results."

Faith's eyes widened. "Really? What does it say?"

"I haven't opened it. I thought you'd like to do the honors."

He handed her the envelope but she pushed it away. "Please, you open it. I wouldn't know what I was reading anyway."

Brandon ripped the envelope open and pulled the

paper out, carefully unfolding it. As his eyes scanned the contents, Faith watched him intently. He was a gorgeous man. She sure would miss looking at him.

"Faith?"

"Huh?"

"Why are you staring at me?" he asked, a crooked smile playing on his lips.

"Sorry. I was thinking about dinner. I might have a salad."

"Alrighty… Anyway, these results are helpful, I think. No connection with anyone who looks to be your birthmother. But, there's someone on here who might be a distant aunt or great aunt."

"Really? So how do we connect that person to my birthmother?"

"This entry looks like it's an older woman, and I don't recognize the name. But, Jackson Parker knows everyone in this town. He's been here his whole life, and he's older than me. Maybe I could pick his brain and see if he remembers this person."

"That'd be great," Faith said. She suddenly felt like she was getting closer to actually finding out the answers she'd been seeking.

"Okay. I'll go see if I can catch up with Jackson then. Thanks for meeting with me," Brandon said as he stood. She suddenly realized she didn't want to go back to Addy's. She wanted to stay there and sit with him all night, even if they never said a word.

Faith stood. "Hey, Brandon?"

"Yeah."

"Thanks for helping me with this. It means a lot."

He smiled, almost sadly, and started walking down the beach toward his house.

∾

BRANDON STOPPED around the corner where she couldn't see him and made sure she got back to her car safely. Chivalry was a part of him, and he wasn't going to let anything happen to Faith. But he couldn't have stood there any longer because his impulses were getting the best of him.

The impulse to pull her into his arms and protect her from anything that might hurt her in life.

The impulse to kiss those pouty, perfect lips of hers.

The impulse to tell her the whole truth about what was happening in two weeks.

But instead, he was hiding behind his neighbor's fence, watching her walk to her car.

He clutched the DNA results in his hand as he started walking down the beach again. Jackson had to know something that could help, and he was determined to find answers.

∾

"GOOD TO SEE YA, BUDDY," Jackson said as he shook hands with Brandon. "Have a seat."

The two men sat down at a small bistro table outside of Jolt. Brandon pulled the paper from his pocket.

"So, I'm going to cut right to the chase. You know Faith?"

"Of course. Great lady. Doing great things at HOPE from what I hear."

"She is. And I'm hoping we can help her with something."

"What's that?"

"Well, Faith actually came to January Cove because she recently learned she was adopted and her birthmother might have been from this area. She had virtually no information, so I had her do a DNA test."

"Like one of those online kits?"

"Right. Anyway, so it came back today and she does have a distant relative. Maybe a great aunt, from what it says here."

Brandon handed the paper to Jackson. "Looks a bit complicated…"

"In a nutshell, there was a woman named Norma Peters. I don't recognize the name."

"Miss Norma. I remember her. She died years ago, though. So she's related to Faith?"

"Looks that way. I don't know how she's related,

though. Do you remember anyone younger than Norma who might have…"

"Oh my gosh." Jackson's face went pale, and he dropped the paper on the table. "I think I know who Faith's mother is."

~

BRANDON'S STOMACH was in a knot. How was he going to tell her this? Would she even believe him? For days, he'd been conflicted on who to tell first. Faith or her birthmother. When Jackson had told him the story, he couldn't believe it. Things like this only happened in movies.

When he saw her walking up to his porch, he wiped his sweaty palms on his pants and opened the door.

He'd told people before that they had a bad diagnosis. He'd had to tell families that their loved one had passed away. But this was way out of his comfort zone.

"Hey," he said as he opened the door.

"Hey. You okay? You look white as a sheet."

"Sure. Come on in."

She followed him to the living room and sat down.

"Why'd you call me here? You seemed a little anxious on the phone."

"Well, I have some news… about the DNA test, actually."

She stilled in the chair, eyes open as big as saucers. "Okay…"

"It's a little shocking…"

"Just tell me, Brandon."

"You're Faith's birthmother, Olivia."

FAITH STOOD AT THE PIER, the wind blowing through her hair. She closed her eyes and took in the smells that only the ocean can produce. She loved that she could literally taste the salt from the ocean water on her lips. January Cove was home to her now, even if Brandon James was leaving.

Maybe he'd get some answers about her birth-mother, at least. Maybe she'd finally get some closure about her earliest moments of life.

Right now, she was confused as to why Olivia had asked to meet her at the pier. They normally met at the office and coordinated the day's events, but Olivia had offered to bring breakfast that they could share at one of the picnic tables at the water's edge.

Olivia had been acting strange lately. Faith worried maybe something was going on in her marriage. Or maybe she was sick. Or maybe she didn't like the job Faith was doing at HOPE. Her mind was swirling with "what if" scenarios that only made her more anxious everyday.

"Good morning," Olivia said with a smile.

"Oh, hey. I didn't see you coming."

"Looked like you were lost in thought?" Olivia said as she put the white paper bags on the table and slid into her seat. "Everything okay?"

"Just thinking about all kinds of stuff. Brandon leaving, the kids at HOPE... the search for my birthmother."

Olivia swallowed hard and smiled. "I get it. Life can get pretty complicated."

"You seem in better spirits this morning," Faith said as she pulled out her fruit cup and muffin. Olivia always knew what to get her. It was weird how she seemed to "get" Faith in a way no one else did.

"I am. I found out some news last night."

"Good news?"

"Very good news. But shocking."

"Oh... do tell," Faith said as she took a bite of her muffin. "I love juicy gossip."

Olivia smiled, but she was definitely nervous about something. So nervous that she dropped her breakfast sandwich on the table, wiped it off and took a bite.

"Liv, are you alright? You seem almost petrified about something."

"I am petrified, honestly." She put down her sandwich and sucked in a deep breath.

Faith reached over and took her hands. "We're friends. I'm here no matter what."

"Oh gosh…" Olivia said.

"Just tell me. You're freaking me out."

She looked at Faith, her eyes welling with tears. "Faith, I'm your birthmother."

CHAPTER 11

$\mathcal{F}$aith sat there in stunned silence as
Olivia looked at her, tears rolling down
her cheeks now. She pulled her hands back and set
them in her lap, unable to form words.

"Faith, did you hear me? The DNA test showed
that my aunt was related to you which can only
mean I'm your birthmother."

"But, how? I mean, did you know all this time?"

"No, of course not! I had no idea until Brandon
told me your story and then your birthday was the
same as Bella's."

"Bella?"

"That was what I named you," she said softly.

"Bella," Faith repeated. It was weird to know that
she once had a totally different name.

"When you found me at the bakery on your
birthday, I was doing what I do every year. I buy a

cupcake, say a prayer for my daughter and then throw it away."

"Why do you throw it away?"

"Because if she can't eat it, then I'm not going to either."

Something about that seemed so sacred yet sad. "So when did you know?"

"I started to wonder when Brandon told me your story, honestly. But I didn't want to get my hopes up. He called me about the DNA last night after talking to Jackson Parker."

"Wait, what did Jackson know?"

"He was one of the only people in town who knew about me being pregnant. I met him at school and confided in him. I was very petite, so no one ever really knew I was pregnant because I just wore baggy clothing to cover it. I ran away when I was seven months pregnant and gave birth in Virginia."

"How in the world did you end up in Virginia?" Faith asked, eager to know the details, but still reeling from the news. She didn't know how to feel.

"I literally ran until I had no money left for bus fare. Gave birth at a hospital there, CPS came and took you and that was it. I don't really know all the ins and outs, honestly. I just knew I couldn't be a good mother to you at sixteen years old. I was terrified if I kept you, you'd end up in the system just like me. So, I signed what they told me to sign and came back to January Cove because it was the only place that actually felt like it could be home. A couple of years later, I finally aged out of foster care and started my life over as best I could."

"And my birth father?"

"Just a one night thing. He took advantage of me being so young, Faith. I'm sorry."

Faith sat there, shell shocked. "You were fifteen when you got pregnant?"

"Yes. I still remember taking the test and telling my foster mother at the time. She slapped me across the face and called me a slut."

"Oh my goodness. That must've been awful, Liv." It felt funny to call her Liv now. Should she call her Mom? That felt weird too.

"It was. I felt so alone in the world. But I had you. I wasn't alone anymore. Those nine months were the most wonderful of my life because you were with me." She reached and squeezed Faith's hands. "I never forgot about you. HOPE was created to help these young kids so they never have to face what I did. And Hope was your middle name, originally at least."

"I don't know what to say."

"You don't have to say anything. This is a lot to take in, for me and for you. I just want you to know that I wanted to keep you more than I wanted to take my next breath. But I was a lost kid myself, and I wanted to break the cycle. And I see now that I did. It was worth all the years of suffering to know that you had a good life, and you turned out to be the most amazing woman."

It suddenly hit Faith like a ton of bricks that she was holding her mother's hands. She began to cry, sob actually, as she felt the weight of her search ending and the enormity of knowing that Olivia was her mother began to hit her.

The two women sat and cried and laughed for a few minutes, no words exchanged between them. Faith stood up, walked around the table and pulled Olivia into an embrace. She was hugging her mother, the woman who actually gave birth to her.

"You're not angry with me?" Olivia finally asked, pulling back to look at her daughter.

"Of course not! Why would I be angry?"

"For abandoning you," Olivia said, tears rolling down her face.

"You didn't abandon me. You did what was right at the time, and I can't thank you enough. As bad as the last year has been, I had a great upbringing. Now I see these kids at HOPE and what my life could've been like had you not made that very difficult decision at sixteen years old. You're my hero."

Olivia smiled and hugged Faith tightly. "You're never getting rid of me again!"

"Ditto!" Faith said with a laugh.

~

BRANDON WAS NERVOUS. Olivia had told him she was meeting with Faith this morning. He kept checking his watch over and over, but time seemed to be passing very slowly. Would Faith be mad that he didn't tell her first?

"Knock knock," he heard Olivia say from the side of his house. She walked around and up the stairs to his deck where he was sitting drinking his third cup of coffee. The caffeine certainly wasn't helping his nerves.

"Hey. So..."

"I told her."

Brandon took in a deep breath. "And? How'd it go?"

"She was shocked, of course, but I think she was actually happy." Olivia was smiling from ear to ear, her eyes still red from what was obviously an emotional meeting with Faith.

"Good. I'm glad it went well," Brandon said, relieved.

"So, listen, I think you need to tell Faith the truth."

"Liv, I can't do that. Not until..."

"I know it's a risk, Brandon, but she thinks..."

"I know," he said, putting his hand up. "But better that she's mad at me than the alternative. I can't do that to her. I'd rather shoulder the burden myself."

"You're stubborn," Olivia said with a laugh as she pinched his arm.

"Takes one to know one."

"True."

"Anyway, I've got an important meeting today. I better go grab a shower."

"Call me when it's over. I'll be waiting to hear."

"Will do," Brandon said. He walked to his back door and turned back around. "You know, I never realized how much our lives would change just because Scooter got loose that day."

"I guess you need to thank Scooter," Olivia said as she walked down the stairs. "I hear he likes filet mignon."

~

FAITH WAS SHELL SHOCKED. She walked around for two days, sometimes smiling and sometimes shaking her head. How was this possible? Was God such a practical joker that he ended up putting Faith and Olivia together through HOPE and then waited for them to figure it out? If so, he had a great sense of humor.

It was already different between her and Olivia. For a day, it felt weird. Awkward, almost. She wasn't sure what to call her. They finally settled on the idea that "Liv" was fine. She might never feel comfortable calling her "Mom" given their close ages, but maybe one day. Whatever happened, they'd be okay with it because they'd found each other.

They'd spent the next evening walking on the beach, talking about their lives and families. Faith had heard some awful stories about things Olivia had gone through, but she'd been inspired by her strength. Even more encouraging was that now she knew she had that kind of inner strength inside of herself. Genetics are a powerful thing.

Faith had shared stories of her storybook upbringing, followed by tales of the takedown of her father. Olivia had asked a lot of questions, wanting to know the most minute details from when Faith had lost her first tooth to the first boy who'd broken her heart. His name was Toby Allgood, she'd told her.

Now, sitting at her desk, Faith stared off into space. The spot in her heart and mind that had been filled with questions was now gone, replaced with visions of a future with her newfound mother. She'd even met Olivia's husband, Ed, who was a super nice guy and a perfect match for Liv.

But there was still a hole in her spirit today as she thought about Brandon leaving soon. She didn't know the details, didn't really want to know. Maybe it'd be better if one day he just wasn't there, had already hopped on a plane bound for the other side of the world. And yet, she knew she wanted to say goodbye, thanks, farewell, see you later, ask him to kiss her... No, forget that last part.

"Don't forget we have to pack those lunches this

afternoon. We have way too many snack cakes, so put two in each bag, okay?" Olivia said as she breezed through the office. "Faith? You okay?"

"What? Yeah. Two snack cakes. Got it."

Olivia sat in the chair across from Faith's desk. "It's Brandon, isn't it?"

"I miss him."

"I know you do. Why don't you go see him? Better yet, why don't you come to a party I'm throwing for him tomorrow night?"

"A party? Is it his birthday?"

"No. It's a... congratulations party."

"Congratulations? For his 'new adventure', you mean?" she asked, using air quotes like a teenager.

Olivia paused for a moment. "Yes."

Faith stood up and paced back and forth behind her desk. "I can't. I'd just be a downer."

"Faith, he helped put us together. The least you can do is just go and support him." Ouch. Motherly advice at its best. Tough and to the point.

But she was right. Brandon had single handedly helped her change her life. She needed to buck up and be the good friend he'd been to her.

"Okay. Where and when?"

"Actually, we're having it at his house tomorrow night at six."

"He's hosting his own party?"

Olivia laughed. "Just using his space. I'm doing everything else."

"Can I bring anything?"

"Just an open mind and that beautiful smile," Olivia said, pinching Faith's cheek before she walked out the door.

An open mind? What did that even mean?

~

FAITH FELT NERVOUS. She hadn't talked to Brandon in days, and she felt bad about that. After all, he'd changed her life by figuring out Olivia was her birthmother. So many times, she'd wanted to call him or go see him to say thank you. But she'd chickened out every time. Not because she wasn't thankful, but because she was afraid she'd beg him to stay.

"Faith, I'm so glad you could come," Brandon said as he opened the front door. He was all smiles, which made her happy and sad. It meant that he was glad to be leaving January Cove to go help people, but it also meant she was losing him.

"Thanks for having me," she said, her stomach filling with a million butterflies. How in the world was she going to say goodbye without breaking down?

"Come on in. Everyone's here."

When she walked inside, the place was packed with people she knew and some she didn't. Of course, the Parker family was in full force with Jackson, Rebecca, Addy and Clay milling about. Addy waved from across the room.

"Hey, Faith! Good to see you!" she said, smiling. Since getting her new job, Faith had finally moved out of Addy's last week and into a bungalow about a block from her office. It was a big change to be alone all the time, but she was loving her new place.

"Good to see you too," Faith said. It really was good to see Addy. She missed seeing her everyday at the inn. "Boy, do I miss your vegan pancakes!"

"I got pretty good at vegan cooking while you were there, huh?"

"Yes, you did!"

"Well, honey, you can come by anytime and eat with us. No invitation required!"

"Thank you."

"So, any idea what this big announcement is?" she whispered, grinning.

Faith swallowed. "Not a clue."

"Brandon seems so excited about it. He can barely keep from smiling."

"Yeah. He does look happy," Faith said, a totally fake smile pasted on her face. She hoped Addy didn't notice that her hands were shaking.

Faith walked to the kitchen where Brandon was standing alone for a moment. "Can I talk to you?"

"Sure," he said, putting his tea on the counter and walking out onto the deck with her.

"Listen, before the festivities begin, I wanted to

say thank you for everything you've done for me. Without you, I wouldn't have found my job or my mother. No matter what, I just wanted you to know that I'm grateful, Brandon." She spit the words out as fast as she could, afraid she'd chicken out or possibly throw up on his shoe if she didn't get them out.

"Faith, you don't have to thank me."

"Yes, I do."

"Brandon, are you ready?" Olivia asked, poking her head out of the door.

Brandon smiled and nodded before looking back at Faith. "I guess it's time for my big announcement."

"I guess so," she said, trying to smile but feeling like running down the beach. Instead, she followed him inside.

Brandon walked to the other side of the living room, and Faith moved next to Olivia across the room from him. This was it. This was when he said goodbye for God knew how long. Maybe years?

"First, I want to say thank you to everyone who came tonight. As you know, I have something exciting to share. It's life changing, and I hope you'll all be happy for me as I take on this new adventure in my life."

Not really new, right? I mean, he'd gone to the Middle East before. Everyone knew that. Faith started to wonder what the big hullabaloo was even about.

169

"A few months ago, I met this crazy woman when Scooter knocked her down on the street…"

Wait. Why was he talking about her?

"Over the last few months, our friendship has meant so much to me. She doesn't realize it, but she's changed who I am as a person. She's also helped me realize what's been missing in my life all these years."

Faith's cheeks were turning red. *Was he proposing or something? Because that would be way out of her comfort zone. Not that she didn't have feelings for him, but that'd be a big jump. From their "almost kiss" to a marriage proposal?*

"Her love for the kids at HOPE and the inner strength she's shown after a really hard few months gave me perspective about my own life."

Where was he going with this?

"A few weeks ago, I made a big decision. I've always wanted to help people. I even went across the world for years to do just that. And I thought that going back there was the only way to help, the only way I could affect lives in a positive way. I thought it was the only way I could contribute to changing this world for the better…"

Wait. He **thought**. *He wasn't leaving?*

"And then one day I realized that changing the world can start right in your own town. In your own home, even. And with that, I'd like to formally introduce you all to…" he said, walking across the room and opening a door in the hallway, "my daughter."

Amelia. Amelia was standing there. She was wearing a beautiful pink dress with the biggest smile on her face. She made eye contact with Faith and waved like a giddy child who just found out they were going to Disney World. Brandon picked her up and she hugged his neck tight as everyone applauded.

Faith felt hot tears rolling down her cheeks. She wiped them away as best she could, trying not to miss any of the scene in front of her. Brandon had adopted Amelia? How? When? She had so many questions, but the sound of applause and cheers pounded in her ears as her heart practically leapt from her chest.

"Everyone, this is Amelia James. She's my daughter, and we're going to take on the world together, aren't we?" he said looking at her. She high fived him as everyone laughed and cheered.

Faith couldn't catch her breath as she watched the scene. Olivia put her arm around her, seeming to notice she was overcome with emotion.

"Surprised?" she whispered.

"Shocked is more like it. Why didn't anyone tell me?"

"Because Brandon didn't want to disappoint you if things didn't work out. He's been working on this for weeks now."

"But I was so mad at him."

"I tried to get him to tell you the truth, but he

preferred you to be mad at him than to be heart-broken if the adoption fell through."

"Oh my gosh... But the texts..."

"Those were from me, Faith. And the notepad was old. Just a bad combination being that they were beside each other."

Faith covered her face. She was embarrassed and mad at herself for jumping to conclusions.

"Hey," she heard Brandon say from behind her. Olivia slipped away into the crowd and left them standing in the kitchen alone.

"Brandon, I'm so sorry I jumped to conclusions."

He put his hands on her shoulders. "It's okay, Faith."

"No, it's not. I was so mad... so hurt..."

"That kind of makes me feel important," he said with a smile.

"You are important. So important that I couldn't imagine you leaving."

"Well, I'm not leaving. I have a daughter to raise."

"I have to know... Did you adopt her for me, Brandon?"

"No. I adopted her because she needed someone who cared. She needed a stable home. And I have the means to raise her in the way she deserves. I realized at the carnival that I could be a great father to her. I've spent a lot of time with Amelia over the last few weeks. We had counseling sessions together, and I took her on day trips so we could get to know each other. I love her. She's my kid. She may not be my blood, but I love her like she is. Her mother decided that it was better to let her be adopted than send her into the foster care system."

"How's Amelia doing with all this?" Faith asked.

"You tell me," he said, looking into the crowd where everyone was swooning over her. Faith had never seen Amelia smile like that. She looked almost angelic as she chatted with the guests and ate a doughnut.

"She looks so happy."

"I think she is. I had her bedroom decorated with princesses. Even got one of those big canopy beds. Almost didn't get the darn thing in the house it was so tall," Brandon said laughing.

"I can't wait to see it."

"I might be spoiling her just a bit," he said, wrinkling his nose.

"She deserves it."

"Miss Faith?" Amelia said from behind Brandon.

"Amelia! I'm so glad to hear this happy news!" Faith said, leaning down and hugging her.

"Thank you. I love it here!"

"I bet you do! Sounds like your Dad is spoiling you rotten already."

"He is, but I like it! Do you want to see my room?"

"Absolutely!" Faith barely got it out of her mouth before Amelia had grabbed her hand and started dragging her up the stairs. It was the first room on the right, overlooking the beautiful ocean view. It was all pink and white and frilly. She couldn't believe Brandon had done this by himself.

"It's beautiful, Amelia. I know you're going to love it here. Look at that view! I'm so jealous!"

"I love to watch the dolphins in the morning. They come up so close," she said, looking out the window and pointing. "Last night, Dad let me eat dessert on my balcony and I saw three dolphins." She held up her little fingers and grinned.

Dad. She was already calling him Dad. Faith's heart swelled.

She turned to see Brandon leaning against the doorframe, smiling. Faith scanned the room and noticed all the little details. A fluffy bean bag chair. A teddy bear almost too big to fit in the room. A tall chest of drawers perfectly painted the starkest shade of white to complement the pink walls. The epitome of a little girl's dream bedroom.

"Did you do all of this?" Faith asked softly as Amelia waved at party guests from her small balcony above the deck.

"I did. You like it?"

Faith walked toward him slowly. "It's amazing, Brandon. You're amazing."

"Amelia?" Olivia called from the bottom of the stairs. "Come get your banana split!"

Amelia flew past them in the doorway and ran

down the stairs. Brandon and Faith were left alone, standing just inside the pink room. With over twenty people milling about downstairs and outside, the volume was loud, but Faith could hear nothing but the ragged breaths she was taking as Brandon closed the space between them.

"You're the amazing one, Faith. You inspired me to do this. Watching you overcome everything these last few months… watching you literally change who you were because you knew you could be a better version of yourself… it made me realize that I could never leave this place again. I could never leave you. It's killed me to have this space between us the last few weeks…"

"It's killed me too," Faith said, a rogue tear rolling down her cheek. "I just couldn't take someone abandoning me again."

He brushed the tear away with his thumb. "I'd never abandon you. And I'll never abandon Amelia. You're my family."

"But we haven't even kissed yet," Faith said with a giggle.

Brandon smiled and slid his hands behind her neck, cradling her head in his hands. "Well, let's remedy that, shall we?"

And with that, his warm lips met hers and Faith McLemore knew she'd finally found her real home - in Brandon James' arms.

EPILOGUE

Six Months Later

Faith pulled the pie from the oven, trying not to burn her hand again. She'd learned a lot of lessons about cooking since being on her own, but the best lesson was not to get distracted in the kitchen and grab a hot dish without an oven mitt. Ouch. Lucky for her that she was dating an ER doc.

"Amelia, honey, have you finished your homework?"

"Almost…"

"You're not playing on your phone, are you?"

"No, ma'am…"

"No pie until that math worksheet is done," Faith called again, smiling at Olivia who was sitting across from her at the breakfast bar. "She'd do anything to get out of math homework."

"Pie is a great bribery tool, though," Liv said,

pinching off a piece of the crust. Faith swatted her hand.

"No pie for you until after dinner," Faith said laughing.

"So where's that fiancé of yours?"

Faith smiled every time someone called him her fiancé. Brandon had surprised her a month ago with a proposal on the beach in front of Olivia, Ed and Amelia. It had been perfect.

"Fishing with Clay." She checked the time on her phone. "He should be home…"

"I'm home!" Brandon called out from the foyer.

"About now," Faith finished her sentence with a laugh.

Faith was still living at her bungalow, but she spent a lot of time at Brandon's. She already thought of Amelia as her daughter, so it was an easy fit. But she couldn't wait to move in with Brandon and Amelia in a few weeks after their wedding.

"Hello, my beautiful bride to be," Brandon said, planting a long, soft kiss on her neck as he entered the kitchen. Faith loved keeping her hair up in a ponytail just to encourage those amazing neck kisses he always gave her.

"Well hello. How was fishing?"

"Clay beat me again. I swear he baits his hook with something illegal."

Olivia laughed. "I think he's just better than you."

"I see I'm already going to have problems with my new mother in law."

"Okay, that's weird. I'm only a few years older than you," Olivia said cringing as if bugs were crawling on her.

"You two stop it or no pie after dinner," Faith chided.

"So, how was your visit with your father last weekend?" Olivia asked, pinching off another piece of pie crust when Faith wasn't looking.

"It was actually really good. He's got a new attorney, and they think they can appeal the case and maybe get him a shorter sentence. I hope it works out. He's done as best as can be expected in there, I guess. He's working in the dining hall, which is funny because he never could cook."

"Was he happy to meet Brandon?"

Faith looked up at him. "He really liked my sweetie. It was just a great visit. A full circle moment. And he was so happy we found each other too," she said, reaching across the counter and squeezing Olivia's hand. "He was glad I finally found where I belong."

Olivia walked around the counter just as Amelia trotted down the stairs. "We are blessed to be family," Olivia said as she hugged her daughter. Brandon, with all his fishy smell, put his arms around them both.

"Hey, what about me?" Amelia yelled as she ran toward them and scooted in the middle of the group.

Faith looked up at Brandon and smiled. Family didn't have to be blood. Sometimes you get to choose your family, and sometimes they choose you. And in that moment, she knew it had all been worth it. Family always was.

~

SEE all of Rachel's books at www. RachelHannaAuthor.com.

CPSIA information can be obtained
at www.ICGtesting.com
Printed in the USA
LVHW100132150322
713463LV00025B/499

9 781953 334541